The Star Riders

Marshal Hal Gunn had always been a solid character – so solid that it seemed nothing could get past his defences. Then, as he returned home to his small ranch on the edge of a vast prairie, his life changed forever. . . .

A ruthless band of Comancheros led by the infamous Tipah Porter had struck. Smoke billowed from the wreckage of his home but there was no sign of his family – only the stench of burning flesh amid the ashes.

Then, just south of the ranch, Gunn caught a glimpse of two horsemen riding along as fast as their horses could carry them. Had the deadly Comancheros returned to finish the Star Riders? There was only one way to find out. . . .

The Star Riders

Roy Patterson

A Black Horse Western

ROBERT HALE · LONDON

ISBN 978-0-7090-9143-1

Robert Hale Limited
Clerkenwell House
Clerkenwell Green
London EC1R 0HT

www.halebooks.com

*Dedicated with eternal gratitude
to the lovely Eileen Gunn*

Typeset by
Derek Doyle & Associates, Shaw Heath
Printed and bound in Great Britain by
CPI Antony Rowe, Chippenham and Eastbourne

PROLOGUE

There are some who appear mighty. Men who seem to be carved from ancient granite. Strong and unbending in their faith and their knowledge that they cannot be harmed. Invulnerable to the slings and arrows which haunt all other living things. Men who are seasoned in all things and totally believe in their own immortality. No others are stronger of mind or fists in the heat of battle. No others can equal their resolve when drawn into a showdown. The belief that they cannot ever be harmed takes root in youth and soon every sinew of their being is filled with this surging confidence.

Like a sabre-waving general at the head of a troop of cavalry they charge on without fear or doubt. For they are convinced that they are blessed by some unseen force. Charged with a power few others could even envisage. Gifted beyond all others. Untouchable or unshakable, they forge on and on where angels fear to tread.

Yet in truth even the mightiest of things can be destroyed by fate, or God, or circumstance. Nothing is immune to the blind fury of things mere mortals can never comprehend. Nothing, not even the stars in the firmament are eternal.

Even towering desert mesas can be brought down from their heavenly heights and turned into mere rubble by the earth at their foundations suddenly moving a mere inch. Tremendous tidal waves can wash away entire islands leaving nothing in their wake except the memories of living things which once dwelled upon them.

Vast forests which have stood for all known time can disappear in a heartbeat when leaping ravenous flames engulf and rampage across their acreage, leaving only ashes behind them. Even huge cities where thousands have lived for generations cannot withstand the unexpected wrath of an erupting volcano. Molten lava and choking dust erupting from the very bowels of Hell can destroy entire civilizations in the mere blink of an eye.

Nothing men have ever devised can prevent disaster and no man ever born has ever managed to get the better of nature.

Yet there are still some men who actually think that they are made from granite. Immune to every tragedy not of their own creating.

It is a delusion.

A mere mirage.

For if life teaches us just one lesson it is that only death is truly certain. Nothing, whether flesh or stone, can withstand the passage of time and the inevitable corruption of years. Even the men who believe that there is nothing which can hurt them eventually learn that simple, brutal lesson.

So it was for Marshal Hal Gunn. The tall, broad-shouldered Texan lawman had never feared anything or anyone in his thirty-eight years of existence. Never once had Gunn been deterred from following even the most dangerous of trails and the most bloodthirsty of outlaws. Like an arrow in flight he had always gone straight and true. Fear was for others, not Gunn.

But even the strongest of men have their Achilles' heel. A part of them which is vulnerable. The chink in their otherwise impenetrable suit of armour. Fate can and does strike like a viper when least expected. Strike and bring down the mightiest of creatures until they are grovelling bewildered upon their knees amid the debris of what had once been their lives.

Hal Gunn was about to learn a lesson.

A valuable lesson.

It would be a cruel one.

Yet like the mythical phoenix Gunn would rise

from the ashes of his own personal despair and become even stronger.

Some men think they are mighty. For a time perhaps they are.

ONE

The blazing light of a new day spread across the red sand as the sun lifted itself up into the vivid blue sky. White skeletal remains of trees and beasts littered this place, markers of death that any sane creature would have heeded. Yet this place, with its burning sand and twisted Joshua trees, had its uses for those who wished to remain lost from the rest of civilization. The Devil, it is said, protects his own. So it was with this unholy place. Here certain men could secrete themselves. For only madmen would venture into this whirlpool of fatality willingly.

There were more than fifty of them. They rode from their sanctuary out across the dry land of the sickening heat like an apparition of impending doom. Half wore sombreros and were laden down with belts of ammunition to feed their arsenal of various weaponry, which was strapped to their lath-ered-up mounts. These were the the most ruthless and dangerous bandits ever to ride from out of the bowels of Hell into the newly settled New Mexico territory. Men who knew that they could never return to the path of rectitude again, even if they had desired to do so. Men who had thrown their lot in with the scum of an array of equally lethal Indians from otherwise noble tribes. Brutal warriors who had defied their own chiefs and set out in a vain attempt to defeat the white intruders who continued to invade their lands no matter how many of them they killed or chased off. These were not Indians from any one tribe but braves who in earlier times regarded one another as enemies equal to the settlers. Riding with the Mexican bandits, they still proudly displayed their various tribal regalia. Apaches, Comanches and Kiowas did not now kill each other but had another common foe upon which to turn their venom. An enemy to whom they showed no mercy.

To all of them it was kill or be killed. There was no other way. They would steal horses and livestock, either to use or to sell to those less capable than themselves. Females were the most precious of commodities though. Females of any age were more valuable than gold. The more settlers who arrived the more they were provided with a constant supply of that most priceless of assets. The colour of their victims' skins did not matter to any of these men, for they knew that the merciless rays of the sun would soon bake them into an acceptable shade of submission.

The leader of the band of unscrupulous riders was himself the result of a union of both white and Indian. Tipah Porter looked every inch an Indian when he wanted to but unlike any of his followers, he had been well educated in missions and, more important, by his mother. The son of a captive white woman, Ann Spring Porter, he soon realized that his heritage would either destroy him or be the one thing which could raise him above all his pure-blood brothers. His sheer intelligence was matched only by his indomitable courage. It was well known that by the time Tipah was only twenty he had mastered not only the various dialects of the Comanche but was fluent in Spanish and English as well.

Knowledge was power and soon Tipah had grown weary of his tribe's elders. He gathered all the hot-headed braves within a hundred miles of the Comanche heartland and set out to find others whom he could turn into a fighting force. The bandits from south of the border were like chickens without heads until they encountered the arrogant Tipah. Soon they, like the warriors who surrounded the young Tipah, were totally under his control. But of all Tipah's qualities it was his unmatched bravery which set him above all who followed him. It set him apart. He could kill without a single twinge of regret.

None of the men he surrounded himself with

dared even to question the tall, handsome Tipah Porter. To do so would be suicidal. Yet why would any of them ever question a man who seemed to be able to think like their enemy? He seemed instinctively to know what any of their enemies would do, even before they knew themselves. No Indian, Mexican or white seemed to be able to do anything that Tipah had not already considered. In only two short years the fifty or so riders had accumulated more cattle and horses, as well as gold coin, to make each of them rich by any standards.

Their raids had also brought them countless captive females to use as slaves in their stronghold. These poor creatures were used not only as objects to debase but as things that they could trade. Tipah Porter also knew that just keeping the females in their encampment would ensure that they were not attacked themselves. For even if their remote desert stronghold were discovered, there was no army that would ever risk killing the very beings whom they wished to extricate.

The riders thundered from the swirling haze of the arid desert behind them and stopped their horses and ponies as one on the high ridge. Dust floated across the men and their charges as they surveyed what lay in the fertile valley below.

The trees along the river's edge had been felled to construct the two buildings which stood close to where a hundred longhorn steers grazed. A couple of horses were corralled close to the larger building, which Tipah knew to be a barn. But his eyes were on the smaller building. Smoke trailed up from the stone chimney and hung in the morning air. He then saw the golden hair of a woman and her offspring glinting in the sun. He nodded to himself.

Tipah turned on his horse's back, then looked to both sides at his men. Each had the ravages of time carved into his brutal features. Yet, like a pack of faithful hounds, they did not do anything but look back to their leader. With a well-rehearsed cry Tipah Porter set his small army into motion. The horses began to ride down the sandy rise towards their goal. The horsemen would encircle both human and animal with the same precision that they had perfected a score of times previously. Like a net cast out from a fishing-boat they would not allow anything to escape them. They would ride wide and then tighten their merciless grip until all was trapped.

Unlike simple rustlers, who also plagued remote regions of the west, this band of hardened, remorseless killers had been branded with a new name. A name which described the blending of Mexican and Indian killers perfectly. A name that was guaranteed to put the fear of God into all who heard it uttered.

These were the infamous Comancheros.

And they were about to strike.

13

TWO

Ezra Withers was old by any standards, yet he still functioned and earned his way on the small ranch owned by his daughter and her husband. Thin as it was possible to be without being planted in a six-foot-deep hole, Ezra had his daily rituals. He knew that whilst his son-in-law, Hal Gunn, was away on his duties as a territorial marshal, it was up to him to be the man of the small family. It was a duty he relished and had never failed to perform since the family had settled in the desert oasis. There was no hint that this day would be any different from the hundreds which had preceded it.

The sprightly Ezra had risen as was his daily habit at just after five. He had fed the hens before filling two pails with warm milk from the cow in the large barn. Now it was just a few minutes after sunrise and he was about to tend the little vegetable patch close to the side of the house. He smiled at his handsome daughter with a pride that only fathers have for their offspring, then beamed even more widely when he heard the sound of his beloved grandchildren Harry and Polly.

Virginia Gunn brushed from the sides of her face the long, golden strands of hair which had escaped the pins she religiously used every morning before starting her chores, and walked to the water pump. She began to fill a bucket with the ice-cold liquid in strong, well-practised movements.

'You OK, Pa?' she asked, as she always asked, as the bucket filled to its brim.

'Fine.' Ezra nodded as he inspected his weathered array of gardening, tools. 'Them kids had vittles yet?'

Virginia blew the persistent strands of hair from her face for the umpteenth time and lifted the bucket. 'Nope. Got the stove fired up, though, and I'll have the skillet ready soon enough.'

'Fine. I could eat me a Sunday feast right about now.' Ezra rested a thin arm on the end of his shovel pole and smiled again. 'The milk and the eggs are waiting, girl.'

'Them hens laying good?' Virginia enquired as her bare feet reached the open door.

'Yep. I picked me up a couple of dozen in the barns.' Ezra had barely finished his sentence when his old blue eyes were drawn to something along the ridge. Something glinting which alerted and alarmed him. He stepped away from the wall and raised a hand to shield his eyes from the sun which was still low and blinding.

No sooner had Virginia entered the house than her two children ran out into the fresh air with their usual loud cries and began to play close to their grandfather. Ezra touched each of their heads in turn as they passed close to his thin frame. Then, as he squinted, he realized what had drawn his attention to the ridge.

Ezra swallowed hard. Yet there was no spittle to moisten his dry, troubled throat. He knew why the rising sun was dancing out there. It had found metal. Gun metal.

The old man clapped his hands together. 'Harry! Polly! Git back inside the house.'

'Why, Gramps?' both children seemed to say at the same time.

Like a shepherd rustling up his flock Ezra guided the two complaining children back towards the only door of the wooden house from which they had just run.

'Inside,' Ezra said. He paused in the doorframe and continued to watch.

'What ya doing, Pa?' Virginia asked. 'I don't want them young 'uns under my feet when I'm preparing food.'

Her father did not reply but remained where he was, blocking the children's way of escape back out into the sunbaked yard.

Virginia looked at her father again. His smile was gone. She felt a cold shiver trace along her spine. She moved from the stove to his side.

'What is it, Pa?' she asked quietly.

'Where's Hal keep that spare Winchester and ammunition, Ginny gal?' Ezra asked as he too felt fear tease his spine.

Her hands gripped his thin bony arm. Her lips moved close to his ear as she whispered. 'What ya seen, Pa?'

His blue eyes flashed at her for the briefest of instants before returning to the unwelcome sight along the full length of the ridge.

'Ain't sure. First I thought it were Injuns and then I thought it were Mexicans. Looks like both but that ain't possible. Is it?'

She bit her lip and moved to the cupboard against the end wall. Her hands pulled out the seldom-used repeating rifle and a box full of shells. 'Ya fasten down the shutters, Pa,' Virginia said in a hushed tone.

Ezra ushered the children toward his small room. 'Play in there. Stay in there.'

He closed the bedroom door and slid the crude wooden bolt across to keep it from opening. He moved far faster than a man of his age should have been capable of to do as his daughter had instructed. In a matter of seconds he had closed and secured the hefty wooden shutters over the two windows which faced the ridge and the uninvited guests, who were now spread out so far in both directions that he was unable to see more than a quarter of their number. They were moving, he thought. Moving out in each direction.

He rested the rifle in the crook of his left arm as his fingers pushed bullet after bullet into the Winchester's magazine. He then rested the box on the hand-made table next to him. He kept on looking at the riders.

They were closer now.

'Can ya see who they are now?' Virginia asked as she moved close to his side next to the open door.

Ezra slowly nodded. 'Yep. I was right. There are Injuns and Mexicans out there. Riding together!'

'That don't make no sense at all, Pa,' the worried female searched vainly for another weapon to use herself. 'I never heard of any Injuns and Mexicans riding together.'

The withered old man knew in his ancient bones that the small army of well-armed riders were trouble. There was no way that men like them intended anything but death to those who stood in their way. He had seen their like before and it chilled him. Cocking the rifle, Ezra knelt on to one knee. 'But that's what they is doing, Ginny gal! They is riding together and we happen to be right in their way.'

Like her father, Victoria had also seen such riders previously and she too knew that death now loomed over their small remote ranch. She moved closer to the bony left shoulder of Ezra as he lifted the heavy Winchester up and closed one eye so that he might focus along its length through the sights.

'They after the stock, Pa? Ya reckon that's what they are hankering for?'

Ezra sighed. He knew that if it were simply one group or the other, she might be right. But to have such different bands of horsemen riding in one group spelled something else. Something he dared not even imagine. He knew of various tribes of Indians who in the past had attacked ranches, not only for the stock but for their womenfolk. Women with fair skin and blonde hair were as valuable as gold in these parts. He did not say a word. He cleared his throat as he kept tracking the riders with his weapon.

'Don't kneel there, Pa. Git behind the door.'

'Ain't easy to shoot accurately from the back of a horse, Ginny,' Ezra informed her. 'I done tried it a lifetime ago. Besides, I ain't gonna be able to hit none of them from behind the door. I have to stay right here.'

19

She gave out a long sigh.

'I knew we should have dug us out a root cellar,' he mumbled to himself. 'We could have put the young 'uns down there.'

Virginia felt the same cold shiver trace her spine as her father had done moments earlier. She went to speak, then felt her throat tighten as though a noose had been secured around her slim neck. Her eyes flashed to the door where her children still played noisily. They were blissfully unaware of what was approaching. She covered her mouth and stared at her brave father. 'This is bad, ain't it?'

'Don't go fretting none, gal,' Ezra said in a tone she recalled from her youth: a strong voice designed to calm her pounding heart. But then she looked at the once powerful figure kneeling there. He was now old and frail and barely capable of holding the weight of the rifle in his arms.

'Pa?' she whispered.

'Easy, Ginny honey! Old Ezra will give them a fight if'n that's what them critters want. Now keep ya back against the wall and let me do all the fretting. Ya hear?'

Her hands smoothed along the old man's shoulders. 'I hear, Pa. I hear good.'

She looked out to the sunlit hillside. Now she could see them clearly. She averted her eyes. It was too frightening to dwell upon. 'Oh, sweet Lord.'

They were closer. Most had swept out after the cattle but at least twenty of their number had headed straight for the two wooden buildings. As they got closer Ezra realized that the Indians were not from just one tribe but several, mixed together as he had never seen them. He recognized the plumage adorning their manes of long black hair.

'Damn it all!' Ezra muttered as he continued to track various horsemen with the long rifle barrel. 'There's Apaches and Kiowas out there. And I seen me a couple of Comanches as well. What in tarnation is going on here?'

'But them Injuns don't even cotton to one another, let alone ride together,' Virginia said, as she heard the sound of the horses' hoofs on the hard, sunbaked ground of their front yard. 'And they is riding with Mexicans?'

'It don't figure,' Ezra said as painted faces of the closest of the braves turned in his direction. 'Damn. They seen me, gal.'

No hoard of diamonds could have glinted more brightly than the barrels of their rifles. The morning sun flashed like warning beacons off the metal barrels as they were aimed towards their target. As the hammers were cocked the sound filled the old man's ears as well as his daughter's.

Ezra squeezed his trigger. The sound of the rifle filled the small wooden building. The children sud-

21

denly stopped making their noise. Before his eyes had recovered from the blinding flash that erupted from his weapon he had cocked the rifle again, but it had been too slow.

As one of the Mexicans was plucked from the saddle of his horse the rest of the Comancheros eased back on their own triggers. No thunderclap in the mightiest of storms could have made more noise. It sounded as though the heavens had exploded.

Every rifle had fired at the open doorway. Every bullet had curled out of their barrels at almost the very same moment. Choking gunsmoke followed the lead. The wall splintered into a million fragments as the door was rocked by the sheer force of the bullets which smashed into it. The smell of burning wood filled the house. Virginia held her hands to her ears and silently screamed. Then she saw the bedroom door open and the two ashen faces of her children framed within its rectangle.

Their eyes were wide as bullets continued to rain down through the open door of the small building.

'Git back in there!' Virginia yelled out above the deafening volley.

Then she saw that their eyes were looking to where their grandfather knelt. Virginia looked at him. He had barely managed to return two more rounds before the rifle bullets had riddled his thin body. Blood flowed from many wounds through the burning cloth on his back. The rifle fell but his bony hands still clutched it. Then he made a sound the like of which she had never heard before.

It was the sound of death.

Virginia reached out to him. He slumped as the flashing rods of death continued to come in from the raiders' rifles. Blood was everywhere. Ezra fell towards his only child. He lay with his head in her lap, upon the apron she always wore. Soon the apron was stained crimson as more and more bullets hit the small, frail man. Now she cradled him as he had once proudly cradled her.

She dragged the rifle from his bloody grip and cocked its mechanism. Now she wanted to kill them. Kill them all. Whoever or whatever they were she wanted to destroy them as they had destroyed her father. There was no other emotion in her body than revenge. Yet the dead old man had her pinned to the floor, unwilling as she was to let him go. She vainly tried to turn to find a target when a cloud of dust was kicked in through the open doorway. Briefly she saw the colourful leggings.

They were upon her.

Virginia Gunn felt something glance across her skull. It brought with it a white flash which filled her head. Then the darkness overwhelmed her as another blow struck her across the top of her golden mane.

She was falling into a place where she did not wish to go, but even as unconsciousness enveloped her she heard her children calling out to her.

Then their cries ended as she felt herself drowning in a whirlpool of black nightmares.

THREE

They had been like a well-oiled machine. The sun had not even reached its zenith above the small ranch set in the lush desert oasis and they were already gone. Yet the evidence of their brief and bloody visitation was everywhere to be seen. They had rounded up all the livestock they wanted and herded it away with the expertise of an experienced trail-drive crew, Only the lingering dust hanging on the dry air bore testament to the Comancheros' having been there at all. That and the blood and fire left in their wake.

Nothing was sacred to these hardened raiders.

That which they desired, they took.

Everything else was laid waste. Even the milk cow was slain because none of the riders knew of its purpose. It was not beef on the hoof like the steers which had grazed along the banks of the narrow river, so it was shot. The productive hens had been used for target practice after the Comancheros had achieved their purpose.

Flames rose high into the otherwise perfect sky as the barn and the house had been torched. The tinder-dry wood was enveloped quickly by the consuming fire, which relished the unexpected meal like a ravenous, living creature and made short work of wooden structures. Only the flesh within their confines continued to feed the fire by late afternoon.

Tipah Porter had overseen everything his followers had done like a general surveying his army on a battlefield. But this had been no noble battle of equals, this had been a slaughter by the mighty of the meek. A massacre. Yet to Porter and his two-legged vermin that was of no significance. They had what they wanted and only one of their number had been wounded in the unholy process.

When Porter had been satisfied that his men had stripped the ranch of everything including its humanity, he had signalled with his rifle and the troop headed back south to their secret encampment with their spoils. A Biblical plague of locusts could not have been more efficient or more ruthless.

Dust lingered as the black smoke wrote pitiful messages on the heavens above the debris. The message would remain into the late afternoon to be read by those who were returning home to discover that no home remained.

*

No funeral pyre could have created a blacker, denser trail of smoke than that which trailed up into the blue sky above the small fertile valley. Even from two miles away its acrid stench filled the nostrils of the two horsemen as they reached the red-sanded foot of a towering mesa. Long dark shadows stretched out across the landscape below them as the burning sun began to dip. They halted their sweating mounts and sat watching as the dust floated away from their animals' hoofs, out over the valley below.

The trees which filled the familiar valley could not disguise the truth from the lead rider's eyes. He stood in his stirrups and tried to suck in air as his teeth nervously ground inside his dry mouth. The younger rider held his gelding in check and stared down to where the smoke was rising with a mind too naïve to imagine the truth of what his friend already knew.

A disbelieving Hal Gunn held on to his reins as his deputy Toby Jones waited for orders. The marshal ran a gloved hand over his face and wiped away the mixture of sweat and tears from his rugged features.

Far below their high vantage point the black smoke continued to rise up from the place that was hidden by the line of trees. It was where his house and barn stood, Gunn told himself silently. He lowered himself down on to his saddle and gathered his reins up until he had pulled the neck of his mount back to where his chest heaved.

'Marshal?' the youngster ventured.

Gunn said nothing. He simply sat and watched the smoke and inhaled the acrid stench he knew only too well. The smell of burning flesh was something you never forgot. The life-span of a man would never be long enough for him to forget that stench once it had filled his nostrils.

'Marshal?' Jones queried again.

Gunn tilted his head and looked at the confused face of his deputy. 'Hush the hell up, Toby!'

The deputy did not say anything else. He just nodded in obedience.

Mustering all his resolve, the marshal gritted his teeth, then rammed both his sharp spurs into the flesh of his horse. He held on for dear life as the faithful animal leapt from the sandy rise and began to gallop down to where the smoke was coming from.

The two star riders left a cloud of dust in their wake as they guided their tired horses down to the valley at breakneck speed. The marshal kept on spurring and whipping the shoulders of his trusty mount with the ends of his reins. The deputy tried vainly to keep pace with his superior but the marshal was being driven by something unknown to the younger man. Jones had never seen Gunn like this before and it worried him.

By the time both horsemen had reached the floor of the valley the marshal was already a quarter-mile ahead of his deputy. Gunn rode like a man possessed by demons. He rode fast and furiously towards the place where he knew his dreams and his heart had been shattered into a thousand fragments.

Every sinew in him screamed out for him not to go to the place he had built with his own bare hands. He wanted to listen and run away so that his memories would not be destroyed, but the star pinned to his chest made him different from other men. It meant he could not simply ride away and hide from the truth, however dreadful that truth might be.

Whatever lay ahead beyond the sickening smoke he had to see it with his own eyes. If it made him throw up like a greenhorn he still had to see it.

There was no alternative.

The horse beneath him began to flag as he got closer to his goal. Gunn drew back on his reins and raised himself from the back of his exhausted mount just as the animal turned into the clutch of trees.

But the hardened Hal Gunn could not have expected to see what his eyes beheld. Even his granite resolve was no match for the soul-destroying sight ahead of him. The long shadows of the late afternoon did nothing but emphasize the horror of the spectacle.

The horse staggered to a halt fifty feet from the blazing ashes of blackened timbers. The flames still licked up from something hidden from sight as the marshal clambered to the ground.

He let go of his reins and began to walk. Then he caught the scent of burning flesh again. He raised his bandanna tails to cover his nostrils but it did not work. The stomach-twisting smell had already entered his nose and would remain there for ever.

Gunn kept on walking straight and true but it was no longer the walk of a confident man, as his had always been. Now he walked with trepidation in every faltering step. It was the stride of a drunken man. Not drunk from hard liquor, but drunk from shock and despair.

Everything he had always held dear in his life was melting inside his brain. He heard Jones rein in and drop to the ground behind him but it meant nothing. He heard the running boots hurriedly approaching him and felt the hand on his shoulder but he did not respond. The hand was trying to stop his progress, but Gunn could not be stopped. His mind was being burned like the wood of his house had been burned. He was unable even to think any longer.

'Don't go no closer, Marshal,' Jones implored over and over again. 'Let me go have me a look!'

Gunn ignored the pleas. The marshal kept on

staggering forward as though he were a fish and was being drawn in by an angler's hook and line. Only the chimney made from stones remained upright amid the smoking ruins.

'Ya don't wanna go see what's in there, Marshal,' Jones yelled out to the man who seemed to be deaf to everything except the pounding of his own broken heart.

'Let me go, Toby,' Gunn snarled like a wild creature, and Jones released his grip.

'But there ain't no good in ya seeing. . . .' Jones muttered as he too inhaled the scent of death and turned away from the flames.

Gunn reached the house. Black timbers creaked as though in greeting to the lawman. He stopped and stared at the smouldering ashes. The roof had caved in before it too had been ignited by the fire. The fire still burned though as it feasted on the flesh hidden somewhere under the pile of blackened ash.

The deputy forced himself to the side of the stunned man.

'What could have happened, Marshal?'

Snorting, Hal Gunn turned and looked to where his barn had stood. It too was still smouldering. Then he saw the dead hens scattered in all directions around the yard. His boots led him to the nearest of the fowls. Pain seared his eyes as he looked down. Jones knelt and picked up the bloody remnants of the hen.

'This chicken has been shot, Marshal!' There was surprise in the youngster's voice. He straightened up and looked at all the others. 'They all bin done shot!'

'Yeah.' Gunn cast his eyes off to where his cattle and horses had been grazing, then returned his attention to Jones. 'This was a raid, Toby boy.'

Jones pointed at the ground. 'There must have bin an awful lot of them, Marshal. Look at all these hoof tracks.'

The marshal did look and saw something his companion had missed. He waved a finger around the red, dusty area.

'Some of them horses were shod and some weren't, Toby,' he ventured before turning back to face the house which was now nothing more than a memory. 'Comancheros!'

Jones gulped. 'Oh, dear Lord.'

Gunn grabbed his deputy's collar and drew him close. His eyes burned into the youngster like branding-irons.

'Don't ya ever go preaching about the Lord to me, Toby,' he snarled. Then he released his grip and staggered back to the ashes. His tear-filled eyes gazed into the smoke. 'If there was a God we'd not be smelling the burning flesh of my family.'

The deputy looked at the ground. Again he nodded.

Oblivious to the heat of the debris, Gunn stepped

into the ashes and began to search. His gloved hands tore away at the charred timbers feverishly.

'Marshal!' Jones croaked as his eyes narrowed as they looked up at the ridge facing the yard. 'Marshal!'

There was a tone in Jones's voice that alerted the seasoned lawman. Gunn straightened up to his full height. He was about to speak when he too saw the silhouettes of two horsemen watching them from the high ridge.

'Ya see them, Marshal?' Jones asked.

Hal Gunn staggered out from the ashes and inhaled deeply. 'I see 'em, Toby.'

FOUR

The sound of vultures filled the air as the huge birds gathered on high thermals above the blood-soaked soil. Ominous shadows flitted across the ground as more and more of their number sensed that death had visited the remote landscape. Yet it was not the hungry birds that had kept the attention of both marshal and deputy. Their eyes were locked on to the two horsemen who were watching the gruesome scene far below their high perch. Even as the sun began to set neither of the riders moved from the place where they had stopped. For what felt like an eternity the two mounted men simply sat and watched.

Both the deputy and Gunn kept their hands firmly gripping the handles of their holstered six-shooters as they squinted up to where the sun was slowly disappearing behind the riders. The sky appeared to be on fire as red hues swept across the heavens beyond the men who watched. The Devil could not have painted a more unnerving picture.

Dust drifted on the evening breeze from the prairie behind the ridge and glowed in the crimson sky. Only the manes and tails of the silhouetted mounts showed any animation. The riders themselves appeared to be little more than statues perched atop their charges.

They sat and they watched.

Jones swallowed hard and stepped back to the marshal's side. At last he dragged his eyes away from the pair of onlookers.

'Who in tarnation are they, Marshal?' the deputy nervously asked, wiping the sweat from his brow along his sleeve. 'What they want? Why they looking down on us like that? If'n they're gonna attack, why don't they up and do it?'

There was a rage burning like a forest fire inside the older man. A rage such as he had never before experienced. Maybe it was the scent of burning flesh behind them which had coiled up inside him like a sidewinder ready to strike. Whatever it was, the marshal wanted to kill. Kill anyone that got in his line of sight. All the years of control seemed to have vanished as grief festered inside his fevered brain.

'They're mocking us, boy.' Gunn spat at the ground where the already stinking carcasses of his hens lay. 'Goading us to waste bullets on them coz they know that even our Winchesters ain't got their range from here!'

'Ya figure them's the bastards that done this, Marshal?' the fearful younger man asked.

'A couple of the vermin!' Gunn snarled. He resisted the urge to draw his Colt and fan its hammer. 'Come to laugh at us as we try to dig out our dead!'

'They're just watching us, Marshal.' Jones sighed. 'Waiting for us to turn our backs.'

Somehow Gunn managed to resist the desire to take wild aim with his weapon at the silent figures on the ridge. He pulled his hand away from his gun grip and clenched his gloved fist. He rested it on his hip and continued to watch them. 'Easy. They ain't got our range either, Toby. If we can't pick them off then they sure can't turkey-shoot us.'

Jones glanced up at the blood-coloured expanse which now stretched along the western horizon. A few stars had already started to show themselves in the brutal red desert sky. Again he looked at the grim face of the man beside whom he stood. It was a face he no longer recognized. It was etched with an anger the deputy had never witnessed before.

'Marshal?' There was the sound of beseeching in the deputy's tone. It asked for something that Gunn no longer seemed to possess. It wanted the solid reassurance the marshal was no longer able to give.

'Ya hear me, Marshal? Are ya sure that they're Comancheros?'

Gunn drew his breath in loudly. His unblinking eyes remained glued to the pair of horsemen, who now seemed bathed in the redness of the sky above them. 'Who else could they be? The critters that killed my family rode off in that direction, Toby! Maybe two of the beggars seen us riding in over the mesa and come back to finish us as well! They're Comancheros OK. Mark my words. That's what they are and I'll kill the both of them given half a chance. They're gonna pay. They'll all pay.'

The outburst of venomous words which spewed from Gunn did not stem the sweat which flowed down Jones's face. The youngster vainly tried to clear his throat, but it was impossible. His face twitched as though nerves were starting to blister inside his terrified mind.

'Y-ya figure that two of them Comancheros come back to kill us as well?' The question splattered from Jones's mouth in one fast gush.

Gunn nodded slowly. 'Comancheros are Indian and Mexican bandits that ride together to steal, rape and kill, boy. And if my old eyes ain't bin tricking me, one of those riders is wearing a mighty-wide-brimmed hat and the other has got himself a damn long mane of hair. Them's Comancheros OK.'

'A Mex and an Injun?' Jones raised his hand to

shield his eyes against the last blinding rays of the sinking sun. He stared hard up at the two horsemen until darkness replaced sunlight and they were gone. 'Are ya sure, Marshal? Are ya?'

'I'm dead sure. And I'll follow them to the ends of the earth until I've killed every last one of the bastards.' Gunn spat again and smashed his right fist into the palm of his left hand.

'I . . . I'll be with ya all the way, Marshal,' Jones said, and nodded.

Gunn diverted his eyes from the now black ridge. He sighed heavily and looked back at the smouldering house. Flames still licked up every now and then from the ash as if defiantly incapable of extinguishing its sickening feast. A feast he knew was the remains of his loved ones.

'Git some kindling and pile it high right there!' Gunn pointed at a bare stretch of the yard six feet from what remained of the house. 'I want light so I can dig out my dead from them ashes, Toby!'

Toby Jones turned from looking at the still burning ruins to gaze upon the ridge, now shrouded in darkness. A cold chill came over him.

'What about them Comancheros?'

'If they come we'll fight,' Gunn muttered. With gloved hands he started to pull away at the hot ash. 'In the meantime I want me a fire. A damn big 'un that'll keep hungry coyotes at bay and also tell us if them two riders head on in.'

Jones nodded. He ran to where they had left their horses and started to gather up as much dry kindling as he could find. When his arms were full he staggered back and dropped the bundle down in exactly the spot Gunn had indicated.

'More kindling, boy. More,' Gunn yelled out without even turning to see how much of the dried vegetation Jones had gathered. 'We need more. More. I want me a damn mountain of the stuff so I can see what's happening. Savvy? If them bastards try to creep down on us we'll be able to see them.'

The deputy hesitated. 'But the fire will let them Comancheros see us real easy as well, Marshal. They'll be able to pick us off like it's a turkey-shoot.'

Gunn turned on him fast. Even the darkness could not hide his eyes from Jones. 'Follow my orders or you'll surely die, Toby.'

'Die?' Jones was frightened. Not frightened by the thought that two of the vermin that had destroyed the ranch and the marshal's kinfolk could sneak up on them, but by the marshal himself. It sounded as though Gunn was now too damn close to insanity to be healthy. The marshal clawed at the hot embers with gloved hands that ignored the heat that burned at the leather.

Yet before Jones could utter another word he saw something which chilled him to the bone.

The older man groaned, then straightened up. The light of a thousand stars illuminated the horrific sight. Jones watched as Gunn walked out of the ashes with the burned body of a child in his muscular arms.

The deputy was shaken not only by the sight of the charred remains but the haunting effect they had on the man he had once considered to be almost emotionless. Jones turned on his heels and ran back to their horses. Yet in his young heart he knew there was no way that anyone could run away from reality, however brutal that reality might be. He paused beside the rested animals and started to gather every piece of kindling he could find. Yet with every beat of his pounding heart he found his eyes drawn to the figure with the smouldering body cradled in his arms.

The sound of the marshal would remain with the youngster for the rest of his days.

No coyote baying at the moon could have sounded more pitiful than did the marshal's howling. It was a sound no man should ever hear another make. Jones swallowed hard as he saw his companion fall to his knees, still cradling the small smoking body in his arms.

Jones stood still. He did not know what to do.

FIVE

Coyotes howled out beyond the tree line. Their chilling sound was enough to make boulders sweat with fear. The smell of death had drifted out on the warm evening air to the animals far beyond the boundaries of the yard. The night seemed to go on for ever. Of the two star riders only one was awake and aware. Toby Jones sat beside the raging fire holding his Winchester in his hands. Every slight noise beyond the range of the fire light drew his instant attention. He had been ordered to sleep but there was no sleep inside him. All he could do was sit and guard his crazed superior.

Marshal Hal Gunn was completely oblivious to everything, including his deputy. His mind had been broken and his heart shattered into a million fragments. With every passing moment the pain grew like a ravenous cancer inside him. Hours earlier Gunn had carried two seared bodies out of the deep ash and laid them out on the sand, but for all his searching he had been unable to find the two others.

The orderly search had become frantic as Gunn hunted for the remaining two corpses. Two corpses that his tormented mind told him had to be there somewhere.

Jones would have suggested that the marshal should rest, or wait for sunrise, but he was afraid to speak to the man who now grunted and snorted like a wild hog hunting truffles. Sanity had deserted the marshal and now the large powerful man was being driven by something else. Something which Jones did not recognize. Respect had given way to fear in the deputy.

In the night sky the stars moved across the heavens. Jones kept feeding the flames of the fire as he had been instructed but now the young man seemed to be unable to feel the fire's heat. It was as though the flames which spat red cinders into the air were devoid of anything except light. Light which danced and played tricks with the weary deputy.

He had been shaking long before the sun had set. He continued to do so even as he sat within inches of the fire's flames. He had lost count of the times he had looked to their two horses, which he had tethered close to what remained of the house. Every few seconds his eyes darted from one sound to the next as his imagination ran riot inside his troubled mind. What frightened the young man the most was the recurring memory of the two horsemen he and Gunn had spied out there on the high ridge before the sun had set.

Who were those two horsemen?

The question kept returning to him.

Was Gunn right? Were they Comancheros? Were they intending to add two star riders to their tally?

It seemed logical, except when you figured that Comancheros were driven by profit. They killed and stole for money. Killing two lawmen offered no profit that the young deputy could think of. He gave Gunn another sad look. The marshal continued to claw at the interior of what had once been a happy home. There was no sense or reason to it any longer but Gunn would not quit. Even if his heart exploded inside his chest, Gunn would not stop.

Jones sighed heavily.

It was a sight which saddened him. The once composed marshal was now more like a crazed creature. He had ripped and clawed away at every inch of the interior of what had once been a house until he was down to bare soil, and still he had not discovered the last two bodies he sought.

Yet Gunn would not cease his search. He could not stop even though it seemed obvious to Jones that if there was something else to find he would have found it by now. The deputy ran a thumb across his jaw and began to think that all the stories he had heard about the ruthless Comancheros were right. They were said to take females either to use or to sell. It was hard to make out who the corpses on the sand were but the deputy sensed they were that of little Harry and old Ezra.

He wanted to tell the marshal of his fears but was afraid even to open his mouth. He had never seen Gunn – or anyone else for that matter – so possessed by demons.

The light of the campfire lit up the fevered search in every sad detail. Jones averted his eyes again.

Then unexpectedly Gunn straightened up and stopped his relentless toil. He was covered in filth but seemed unaware of anything. He staggered out from the blackened dirt and moved towards the campfire and the place where the two burned bodies lay. Jones watched his every move but the marshal did not notice him. Gunn tried to fight his tiredness but it was pointless. He fell on the ground next to the twisted remains and began to sob. Then, at last, exhaustion overwhelmed the marshal and he fell into a deep sleep.

Jones looked up at the stars once more.

'Thank the Lord,' he muttered.

Then he heard a noise. For the first time since he had lit the dry kindling he did not jump into action and swing around with the barrel of his rifle to where he had heard the sound. There had been so many noises that he no longer believed that it had to be the two riders moving in on them.

Jones felt himself yawn. He blinked hard and gave the marshal a glance. He knew that Gunn needed rest if he were ever to regain his sanity. The deputy moved his head until he heard his neck click.

He placed the rifle on the ground, rose up on to his knees and reached forward. He picked up a couple of logs and threw them into the flames. He watched as sparks rose up into the sky. As the flames steadied themselves before his tired eyes he noticed something through the colourful flare-ups.

Like a curious tired child he got to his feet, took a few steps and screwed up his eyes to see more clearly. Again the sound of things all around him out there in the darkness made his eyes dart in all directions. He yawned again and walked to where the marshal lay, virtually unconscious.

The thought of getting their trail blankets from the saddles and covering the sleeping man came to him at the same moment as the light of the fire drew the deputy's attention. Jones froze to the spot.

Out of the darkness something was moving towards him.

Something which the light of the fire was illuminating. At first his burning eyes did not comprehend what they were focused upon. Then the truth smashed though Jones's fatigue.

Toby Jones felt his heart tighten inside his chest.

The sight of the tall stony-faced Indian stopped the deputy in his tracks. He felt himself pant as fear engulfed him. He looked at his hands. Then he recalled that he had left the Winchester on the ground.

No matter how many times he blinked the vision would not disappear. The light of the campfire washed over the man who was silently approaching. The Indian was huge. The closer he got the bigger he became.

Jones knew he ought to go for his holstered Colt. Everything told him to go for his gun but his hands were paralysed. He wanted to call out at the figure and tell him to stop but he could not utter even the quietest of words.

Instinctively Jones backed away with faltering steps. He was terrified. His eyes darted to the sleeping marshal. The deputy wanted to call out and warn Gunn but again he could not utter a solitary word from his open mouth.

He kept backing away. His wide-open eyes were fixed upon the huge man, who had no expression upon his face. The Indian was clad in buckskin which covered his entire form apart from his hands and head. It was unusual in this climate at this time of the year to find any Indian so completely covered.

Although the deputy did not know it, he was looking at an Apache brave. A darn big one. Jones kept retreating from the silent figure who moved silently at him.

Was this one of the men who had destroyed Gunn's family?

The question burned into the youngster. He wanted to avenge the marshal's dead. Even terrified, he wanted to try and kill at least one of the vermin who had done this awful thing.

Toby Jones began to raise his right hand up to where his gun rested in its holster high on his hip. With each backwards step his hand inched up to the holster. The flickering light of the campfire began to dance across the huge Indian. Jones could see that the hooded eyes were tracking the progression of his hand.

Then another question screamed inside Jones's head. If this was one of the Comancheros, why hadn't he simply shot both Gunn and his deputy from the cover of darkness?

Was this some strange monstrous ritual? Some perverted way of making the killing acceptable to whatever rules the Indian and his fellow raiders lived by?

Then as the deputy stepped over his rifle he felt something suddenly stop him. Something which had found the bottom of his spine and was being held firmly.

It was a gun barrel. Jones stopped and blinked slowly.

He knew that his retreat had located the second of the riders whom he and Gunn had seen up on the ridge. The cold steel of the gun barrel pushed into his back with a short movement.

Without even realizing it, Jones raised his hands and arms high. It was a motion he had witnessed so many others do when confronted by the marshal. It was something which he had never thought he would have to do himself.

The large Apache warrior continued to walk towards him. It was only when the brave was standing within spitting distance that the youthful law officer became fully aware of exactly how tall the silent Indian actually was. Jones knew that he himself was close to six feet in height but the Apache towered over him. He had never seen anyone as tall before and it chilled his soul.

Jones felt his heart quicken its pace as he fully expected the mute man to kill him within a matter of moments. The deputy saw the holstered gun on the Apache brave's right hip and a large knife on the opposite one, hanging in a beaded sheath. Death was close and Jones knew it. Either the gun pressed into his spine would blow his back apart or the warrior would dispatch him with either of his own weapons. Again Jones looked to Gunn for help but the sleeping star rider had his own nightmares to handle.

The brave moved. Fearing the worst, Jones closed his eyes and gritted his teeth.

The Apache moved like a striking rattler and snatched the deputy's gun from its holster. Without any hint of emotion he tucked its barrel into his belt before he stepped back and folded his arms. There was still no expression.

'W-what ya figuring on doing?' Jones asked the Indian as beads of sweat traced down his face from his hatband. 'If'n ya gonna kill me then do it. I ain't feared.'

Then a voice came from behind Jones's shoulder. It was a low calm voice, flavoured with a Mexican accent.

'Tahoka is not going to do anything, *señor*,' it said.

The deputy swung around to face the man who spoke. To his surprise he was faced by a handsome, smiling figure clad entirely in black. The man was somewhere in his late twenties and was holding a gleaming silver pistol in his left hand. The sombrero was adorned with silver thread embellishment. The smiling Mexican walked to the fire and raised his free hand to warm it. He looked hard at the sleeping marshal, then back at the confused deputy.

Jones looked at both men. A Mexican and an

Indian. Just like Gunn had warned him.

'Ya stinking pair of Comancheros, why'd ya kill the marshal's family?' the deputy blurted. 'Innocent kids and—'

'We are not Comancheros, *señor.*' The man with the silver gun told him. 'We did not do this.'

Relieved, Jones felt his face start to twitch again as a strange pain clenched into his spine. He lowered his head and watched his sweat drop into the sand at his feet. He panted like an exhausted hound for a few seconds before looking up at the handsome Mexican again. 'Then who the hell are ya? What ya playing at?'

The Mexican raised an eyebrow. 'I say again, we did not kill anyone, *señor.* Tahoka and I were drawn here from out on the prairie by the smoke.'

Jones straightened up. 'Ya ain't Comancheros?'

The expressions on both men's faces hardened.

'I can assure you that we are not Comancheros, *señor.*' The man beneath the black sombrero spat at the ground in disgust at even having to uttered the word. 'They are the lowest of the low.'

The deputy swallowed hard and pointed at the Apache. 'How come he don't talk? He just stares with them evil eyes of his.'

'It is hard to chatter when you have no tongue, *amigo,*' the Mexican said in a low tone. 'My little elephant speaks with his hands when he wishes.'

'How can I believe ya ain't Comancheros?' Jones clutched at the back of his neck. 'An Injun and a Mexican riding together, I thought that meant ya was—'

The silver barrel of the pistol suddenly pushed into the mouth of the distraught deputy. It silenced him. The handsome man then lowered and holstered the weapon. 'You ask how you can believe me, *amigo*? You are alive and that is all the proof I can give you. We could have killed you many times but that is not our way.'

Jones pointed at the bodies. 'Look what they done. They killed and then burned them like they was nothing.'

'We shall help you and your fevered *amigo*.'

Jones was totally confused. 'Who are ya then?'

The handsome Mexican pointed to his silent friend. 'He is Tahoka. I saved his life many years ago and since then he is like my shadow.'

'And what they call you?' the deputy pressed.

'I am Zococa.'

The deputy's eyes widened. 'The bandit?'

'*Sí*!' Zococa smiled. 'The famous bandit who wants to help you and your *amigo*.'

'Why would a couple of bandits wanna help us?' The deputy looked at both of them in turn. 'Them Comancheros are bandits and you'd go up against ya own kind?'

Zococa sighed. 'They are not our kind. We do not hurt the young or the old or the weak. I have been blamed for many things I did not do. No, my young *amigo*. We are not like those who did this.'

Toby Jones crouched down and grabbed a handful of sand. He watched as it trailed through his fingers. His eyes then found the face of the bandit once more. 'Why'd ya wait so long to make an appearance, Zococa? Ya was out there watching us for the longest while.'

'If Tahoka and I had ridden down here earlier we would have surely died or been forced to fight you both, *señor*,' Zococa said drily. 'Your *amigo* has been loco with grief. Even from the ridge we could sense that. We waited until it was safe.'

Then all of a sudden Hal Gunn swung around and pulled the feet of the huge Apache from under him. Tahoka fell on to his back heavily. He was winded. The marshal scrambled to his feet and drew his Colt from its holster.

'Comancheros!' Gunn boomed.

'No, Marshal,' Jones bellowed out as he saw and heard the hammer of the .45 being cocked for action.

Sand fell from the marshal's clothing as Gunn snarled and waved the weapon around.

'Hush up, Toby boy. I got me some killing to do.'

SIX

Jones grabbed at the sand on the ground and raised himself up on to his knees. The light of the campfire illuminated his distraught features as he hollered out at his boss.

'No, Marshal. No.'

'I told ya to be quiet, boy. Listen up.' Nothing looked like the face of the marshal as he waved the deadly Colt at the motionless bandit and the winded Apache who was lying less than a yard from the blazing edge of the fire. Gunn was soaked in his own sweat as he wavered forward.

'This ain't right,' the deputy yelled out. He knew that there were few men as deadly with a six-shooter as the marshal. 'Don't kill 'em. They ain't what ya thinks they are.'

Gunn gritted his teeth, then slowly raised the .45 until it was at arm's length. His face twisted as he

53

stared along his arm and down the barrel of the Colt. All he could think about now was the need to avenge the atrocity evidenced behind his broad back, to destroy those who he believed had taken part in the mindless massacre of his family. His index finger stroked the cold steel trigger of his weapon in anticipation.

'They're already dead, Toby boy. All of them stinking Comancheros is dead,' the star rider declared. 'They bin dead ever since they done this. I ain't killing 'em I'm just giving them what they give Virginia and—'

Without even knowing exactly why, Toby Jones swung his arm with every ounce of power he had and propelled the handful of sand up into the face of his superior. Gunn recoiled as his eyes filled with the burning grit.

A rod of blinding lightning spewed from the gun barrel and exploded into the air as the deputy leapt like a puma across the distance between them and grappled with the unsteady marshal. Though the marshal was by far the more muscular, Jones brought him down. As they landed on the sand the .45 went flying from Gunn's grip. Jones swung around on the sand and kicked the gun away as a fist caught him squarely on the jaw. The deputy was stunned by the sheer force of the blow but held on to the marshal as they rolled around close to the edge of the blazing fire.

Punch after punch rained into the face and body of the younger man from the raging Gunn but Jones held on. He knew that he could never defeat the marshal but he had to try and subdue him. The two men rolled over into the ashes, yet neither of them seemed to notice. No matter how many blows Gunn unleashed on his deputy the youngster refused to return punches. A cloud of sparks rose from around them as they rolled across the heart of the fire and back on to cold sand.

'I'll kill ya!' Gunn screamed out.

The bloodied and battered deputy said nothing back. It was all he could do just to hold on to the man who seemed to have the strength of a stampeding bull. Jones felt another punch catch him in the guts. It hurt and the taste of blood filled the deputy's mouth. Jones clung on and spat at the sand.

'Let go, ya young bastard,' Gunn yelled out again. 'What ya trying to do?'

Gunn punched his way free and managed to get back on to his feet. It was an exhausted Jones who swung his right leg sideways and took the feet from under the marshal. As Gunn crashed on to his back the deputy threw himself on top of him and vainly attempted to keep him there.

The marshal put both his hands under the deputy and hoisted him off. Jones flew backwards like a rag doll. But the deputy was not about to quit. He scrambled back to Gunn before the larger man had time to get back up. They wrestled on the sand for another few moments before the marshal tossed the youngster aside and forced himself back to his feet. He turned and sank his boot into the belly of the deputy. Jones curled up in agony. This time Gunn knew that Jones would not be able to continue his fight.

Swaying like a man drunk on grief, Gunn clawed at his burning eyes until he managed to rid them of the excruciating sand. He blinked hard and long and glared through the waterfall of tears which flowed from his eyes.

'Where's my hogleg?' the marshal snarled as he desperately looked for his weapon around the ground at his feet.

He looked up. Then he saw them clearly.

Standing next to one another Zococa and his trusty companion watched as the marshal plodded towards them with clenched fists.

'I'll kill ya both with my bare hands,' Gunn roared.

Zococa shook his head. 'We did not do this, *señor*.'

As Gunn's hands reached for the handsome bandit's throat he felt himself being lifted off the ground by the Apache's powerful hands and arms. Tahoka held the man in his grip as though Gunn were weightless. The warrior's glance found his partner as Zococa gave his friend a silent instruction with his left hand.

Immediately Tahoka dropped the lawman.

Gunn was breathing hard as he rested on one knee and looked at the two men before him. His attention then went to Jones, who had managed to clamber to his feet. The deputy walked unsteadily towards the small group. Blood covered the deputy's young face.

'Traitor!' Gunn screamed. 'Ya helped these killers. I'll never forgive ya for that, boy. Never forgive ya. Hear me, boy? Do ya?'

Jones paused above the kneeling man. He wiped his face with his hands and rubbed the gore off on his shirt. 'Ya got it wrong, Marshal. These men ain't Comancheros. They never done this.'

'Is that the lies they fed ya?' Gunn growled as his fist pounded on his knee as though it were a war drum. 'Look at them, boy. What else would they be but Comancheros?'

'They could have killed us darn easy, Marshal,' Jones said. 'But we ain't dead. Think about it, Marshal. These men ain't responsible for any of this.'

The lawman still growled. 'Then what they doing here, Toby boy? What lies they poisoned ya with?'

'They seen the smoke just like we done.' Jones sighed and ran the back of a sleeve across his bloody jaw.

'Can't be true.' Gunn looked at the faces of the men who stood before him. He could not understand anything any longer. His head shook as he tried to fathom what was happening to his once perfect life. 'It's some kinda cruel trick. Has to be a trick.'

'It ain't no trick,' Jones insisted.

Zococa gave his tall partner a quick look. Although no words passed between them Tahoka seemed to understand what the bandit was instructing him to do. The warrior turned and walked back into the darkness as silently as a big cat stalking its prey.

'Where's he going?' Gunn asked, staggering back to his full height. 'Where's that damn stinking Injun going?'

Zococa did not answer the question but posed one of his own. The tone of his voice was like a honed razor.

'Do you wish for Tahoka and me to help you find those who did this terrible thing, *señor*?' he asked quietly as he toyed with the drawstring of his sombrero.

Gunn ran his fingers through his sweat-soaked hair. He glanced at his deputy, then back at the bandit. 'What ya asking me? Ya wanna help?'

Zococa tightened the drawstring, then nodded. '*Sí, amigo*. We want to help you find your wife and child. To save them before bad things happen to them as well.'

The marshal stared hard at the handsome face and pointed back at the smouldering remnants of what had once been his home. 'They're dead, boy. Dead in there. I just ain't managed to find them yet.'

'They are not dead,' Zococa announced firmly. 'My little elephant can read the tracks on the ground even in the darkness. He told me that a woman and a little girl were taken from your house by the vermin who did this. The Comancheros have them and are probably taking them to their lair.'

'Not dead?' Gunn blinked hard.

'But I thought ya said he couldn't talk, Zococa?' Jones queried as his superior absorbed the bandit's words. 'He ain't got no tongue.'

Zococa raised both his own hands. 'He uses his hands to speak to me, *amigo*. He might be mute but he is the best tracker on either side of the border. If Tahoka says that the Comancheros took a woman and child then that is what happened.'

Hal Gunn inhaled deeply and tried to compose himself. 'Ya said a woman and a little girl were taken from the house? How'd ya know it weren't a little boy?'

Zococa looked at the ground. 'Comancheros would only take females, *señor*. The male child is not worth anything to those who buy and sell people.'

The older star rider cupped his face with his hands and shook his head again and again. Then he looked down at the burned corpses he had found hours earlier. 'Then that little 'un is my Harry.'

'*Sí, señor.*' Zococa swallowed hard.

Jones stepped closer to the marshal. 'Leastways we now know that Polly and ya good lady is alive.'

Gunn exhaled loudly. For the first time since he and his deputy had arrived back at the ranch he felt as though he were starting to regain control of his sanity.

'How we gonna do this, Zococa?' Gunn asked, staring at the burned remains. Remains that he had to bury deep.

'Do what, *señor*?' Zococa stepped away from both star riders and looked out to where he knew his companion waited with their horses.

'We gonna ride together after them varmints?'

'First my little friend and I have to find them,' the bandit replied.

'How will me and Toby find ya?'

'We shall find you, *señor*.'

Gunn rubbed his filthy hands down his shirt. 'I'm a big enough man to admit when I've bin wrong. I wanna thank ya, Zococa.'

There was no reply.

Both star riders turned to where the bandit had been standing less than a minute before.

Zococa was gone.

The sound of two horses galloping away filled the

ears of the marshal. Gunn gripped his deputy's arm.

'Find a shovel, Toby boy. We better bury old Ezra and little Harry before the sun comes back up.' The marshal sighed.

'Sure enough.' Toby Jones wandered to the side of what had once been a wall and searched for the gardening tools he had seen Ezra Withers use so many times. 'Then are we heading on out after Zococa and his pal, Marshal?'

Gunn looked at his deputy. 'I reckon we'd better head on over to El Diablo first, son. We might need to rustle us up a posse.'

Toby found a shovel and walked back to where his square-shouldered superior was standing. 'But what if that Zococa can't find us, Marshal?'

The lawman sighed and raised an eyebrow.

'I got me a gut feeling that those two *hombres* will find us wherever we is, Toby.'

'Yeah. Me too.' Jones nodded in agreement.

SEVEN

Clad in his colourful warrior trappings, Tipah Porter rode at the head of his men and their plundered spoils like a medieval king triumphantly returning from the crusades. His caravan was big, even by their standards, for the Gunn ranch had not been the only victim to taste the brutal venom of his followers. A herd of 1,000 longhorn and white-faced cattle moved along to the left of Porter, whilst 200 horses of various quality kept pace with lowered heads in a long remuda to his right. A prairie schooner travelled dead centre of the combined herds of steers and horses that the Comancheros had accumulated. This contained the female hostages whom Porter's men had plucked from the various ranches during their unholy crusade. Virginia Gunn held her petrified daughter close to her bosom and stared at the other females inside the covered wagon. Sweat trailed from each of them and only the canvas stretched over the wagon bows gave them any relief from the merciless sun.

The Comancheros had travelled throughout the hours of darkness and continued their stiff pace as the sun rose to herald another day. None of the hardened bandits had wished to stop to feed. Their canteens supplied all they needed until they reached their goal. Mile after mile they had pressed on through the prairie until they had been faced by the barren desert of mountains and sand.

Most sane men would have turned away from a place which seemed to offer only death to those who entered its confines, but not Porter or his followers. To them this lethal land was a sanctuary. They knew it better than most and had found out its secret beyond the walls of white sand. The flowing dunes crept to ensnare the naïve and weary. Bleached bones marked almost every flat space between them but the caravan continued on. Unlike all others who had ventured to this place, Tipah Porter and his men were unafraid.

It had protected them from all intruders for years. None of the Comancheros had any doubt that it would keep doing so for as long as they desired it.

The land began to dip ahead of them. Porter knew that they were heading downward into a valley so vast and covered by towering dunes that the temperature would almost double before noon. Yet beyond that place of roasting heat there lay a miracle. A miracle which, Porter knew, could sustain them for an eternity if they chose to remain there.

Porter waved his rifle at his most trusted men, Cole Jardine and Red Sky, who had been leading the herd of steers. Both horsemen rode to him as Porter pressed ever onward. Jardine had been standing on a gallows platform with a rope around his neck five years earlier in Waco when Porter had freed him by sheer force of numbers. Jardine was the only non-Mexican to ride with the infamous Comancheros. The outlaw owed Porter a debt and liked it that way. He steadied his horse next to his saviour.

Porter looked at Red Sky and Jardine in turn. 'It's time to drive the herd across the border to that fat general and get our dues, Cole. Take ten of the men with ya and meet up with us at the hideout.'

Jardine and Red Sky returned to the herd and headed them away from the wagon and the horses.

The eagle feathers upon Tipah Porter's war bonnet no longer moved on his wide back. Now there was no breeze to cool any of them, but they pressed ever onward.

The prairie slowly dissolved into a swirling heat haze of nothing but sand. White-hot sand set against a canvas of blue cloudless sky was all there was for what appeared to go on into infinity. The high mesas were left behind as marker posts for the travellers who ventured beyond this point. For beyond this place there was nothing except death. The trail had twisted and turned down into a deep gorge, which was as wide as any valley known to the riders. The cactus and sagebrush had become smaller the further on into the satanic oven of burning air the two horsemen rode. Wherever they looked there was only white sand beneath a blue to match any ocean. Nothing else. It was said that only the loco rode beyond this point, but the pair of riders were not insane. They rode on because that was where the churned-up sand told them others had gone before. The others for whom they were searching.

The sand was cut up for a hundred yards to either side of the two riders as they drove their mounts on into the burning air. It alone was proof that the fifty or so Comancheros had driven their captured bounty this way. Cattle and horses left a mark on the land like no other creatures. Their hoofs had ploughed the deepest of furrows in an otherwise pristine landscape.

The trail was clear, yet neither horseman trusted it, or those who had left their mark. The bandit pulled back on his reins and stopped his mighty pinto stallion. He raised a hand to shield his eyes and stared out into the sunbaked ocean of sand ahead of them.

The Apache did not seem to feel the heat like his partner, but there was no mistaking the concern carved into his jagged features. Even Tahoka did not trust the route that their tracking had followed for nearly seven hours. The warrior wrapped his reins around his saddle horn and spoke with his massive hands.

Zococa gave a slow nod. He understood every unspoken word.

'You are correct, my little one,' the bandit said as he stood briefly in his stirrups to survey the land that surrounded them. They were like two small islands in a vast white sea. A sea as perilous as any flowing off the shores of this great continent. 'I am also thinking that we are being lured to our coffins by the men who left this trail.'

Tahoka pointed to the west and nodded hard and forcefully.

The bandit shrugged. 'It is true that El Diablo is only ten miles away but the tracks tell us the Comancheros went south. I do not see what we would gain by heading to that small town, *amigo*.'

Again the Indian spoke with his hands.

A broad smile filled the face of the bandit. 'You are very clever, my little one. I think you have learned a lot by riding with the great Zococa. Come. We go to El Diablo and await the two star riders.'

Tahoka gestured.

The bandit nodded. '*Sí,* little one. They will go there to buy provisions and seek men to ride with them, but I think the old one will be disappointed. The men in El Diablo are not courageous like us.'

Both horsemen thundered across the white sand towards the small border town known as the home of the Devil himself.

EIGHT

Everything within a hundred miles was tinder dry. Without the underground supply of fresh water not even sidewinders could have survived beneath the remorseless sun which beat down upon the array of buildings that was El Diablo. The bowels of Hell itself could not have been hotter or more vile to the eyes and noses of civilized folks. The stench of its outhouses greeted all who rode towards the wild settlement, but there was another even more telling aroma that alerted strangers to what El Diablo held in store for the unwary or naïve. It was the acrid scent of gunsmoke.

There was hardly a moment of the day or night when guns and rifles were not fired into the air or the bodies of others. Celebration and showdowns and just downright murder kept the smell fresh in every nostril. Then there was the boiling blood of the hapless, which quickly turned into a sticky mess only seconds after being spilled. It too had a fragrance that was never forgotten.

There was a saying that some men left their mark on all they touched. Perhaps it was more accurate to say they left their scent. Putrid air choked all but those who had grown used to it for miles in every direction. El Diablo was a weeping sore on the scorched landscape of the south-west. Those who lived in or around the sprawling town were the dregs of humanity and wanted nothing more than the crude life this place offered them and their kind. There were plenty of heavy gambling, hard liquor and loose women to last a lifetime in El Diablo. Not that lives lasted too long in any of the towns which were scattered along the uncharted border. Life here was cheap. Damn cheap.

A seven-cent bullet was all there was between a winning poker hand and a freshly dug hole up on Boot Hill. Seven cents was about all any of the good-for-nothing lives was worth in El Diablo and for some that was being mighty generous. A festering ulcer had more claim to survival than any of those who frequented this unholy town. They lived by the most basic of instincts and nothing apart from themselves had any value.

Its menfolk were little better than the outlaws they regularly did business with. Its banks were filled with the loot of the lowest forms of creatures. No questions were asked in El Diablo, for the answers came too close to the truth for any of the high hats to stomach. The females were all cut from a very soiled cloth; they also lived for the moment, because they knew the brutal reality of this town. Their gender offered them even less protection than the men they serviced.

Few married women lived anywhere close to the border town, for they knew better. Their sort were not wanted by the men who lived their lives fast because they knew it would not last long enough for any of them to get tied down. The creatures who did exist within the unmarked boundaries were those who could never exist in decent company.

Driven further and further west by the creeping civilization that always spoiled men's pleasures, they all knew there was nowhere else they could go. This was the end of the trail to all who refused to buckle to progress. There was only one more stop any of them would take from here and that was Boot Hill.

In only a matter of decades, town after town had sprung up across the vast land known as the Wild West. Simple tents gave way to wooden and brick buildings. It was always the barbers who arrived first, alongside the gamblers and the whores. Then, when the shooting eased up a tad, the spoilers always turned up with a law book in one hand and a Bible in the other. The spoilers brought law and churches and destroyed the very reason for the towns' original existence.

So far that had not happened to El Diablo. So far its very situation in the heart of an otherwise deadly location had protected it from the spoilers. So far it remained what it had always been.

A cesspit.

The law had tried and failed to take El Diablo by the scruff of its neck many times, but the law had always been wrecked before it had had time to take root. With a gun in his hand and a plentiful supply of seven-cent bullets even a coward was brave enough to walk the unnamed streets of El Diablo.

The town was an agglomeration of whitewashed adobe buildings with just a few wooden edifices at its centre. The streets had no formal design. A spider's web had more design. The wooden structures had been brought in and erected by the gamblers who wished to benefit from the town's rugged reputation. Like the banks filled with outlaws' spoils, they had prospered. There was money to be made in places like El Diablo. An awful lot of money and most of it bloody. The place was a mixture of the worst from both sides of the border. It seemed to exist on gaming-halls and saloons, balanced with a plentiful supply of brothels dotted in between.

Men made and lost fortunes in El Diablo. Men

knew that if you had the guts to bring in a supply wagon filled with provisions you could become rich within a heartbeat. You could also become dead just as quickly.

Whatever laws men lived by in the outside world meant nothing here in the dusty sun-bleached streets. Courage and the ability to bluff were the only things that protected you in Hell. That and a lot of cheap bullets.

To face street after street of demons meant you had to be more devilish than the next man. You had to do business the way most played poker.

The only instinct anyone needed in El Diablo was the precious one of survival. That and the ability to kill without thought or regret.

A cloud of dust traced from the hoofs of the two horses as their masters reined in and studied the town to which their flared nostrils had alerted them many miles earlier. Zococa held on to his reins and steadied his pinto as his companion watched every movement with darting eyes. The huge Apache brave began to gesture with the fingers of his free hand, then he pointed.

The bandit gave a slow nod as his own eyes focused on a twisted body lying less than twenty feet from the trail into the town. The body lay curled as though dried by the sun. A large circle of blackened sand surrounded the body. It was blood, baked by days of exposure to the elements.

'The people here do not seem to be in a hurry to bury their dead, my little one,' Zococa remarked. 'Even the buzzards have left that poor fool for fresher pickings, I think.'

Tahoka gestured that there was another dead body ahead of them, somewhere beyond the first of the many houses. His hand dropped to the grip of his gun and he pulled the weapon from its holster.

'Easy, Tahoka,' Zococa said as he watched the Apache check that his Colt was fully loaded. 'Remember that we are bandits and this town is filled with other less famous bandits.'

The eyes of the warrior continued their vigilance as he reluctantly slid his weapon back into its leather cradle on his right hip. A series of shots rang out far ahead of them. Then the town seemed to go silent once more. The bandit patted the troubled shoulder of Tahoka.

'Come, my valiant one.' Zococa tapped his spurs and led the way into the heat haze. 'We shall find the man who thinks he is the boss of this town and then we shall educate him. Before sunset I shall be able to execute my plan.'

They kept a slow pace as their horses rode into the outskirts of the infamous settlement and headed to where they felt the centre of the town had to be.

They had not seen many souls as they had passed

the first of the white buildings but the further they rode the more eyes they knew were upon them. Tahoka had been right about there being another body ahead. They rode past it and ducked as a handful of buzzards lifted off the ground momentarily before returning to their feast.

The narrow lanes twisted and turned. The bandit saw the heads of many people in the open doorways of the houses. They were all watching them.

Any visitors to El Diablo drew attention.

For here humanity had become little better than leeches. They wanted to suck the blood from any stranger who dared risk their wrath. The females painted their faces with yet another coat of colourful make-up just in case the riders wanted to enjoy their services. The gamblers broke the seals on fresh packs of cards in case the men were gamblers. The saloon-keepers polished the dust from the bottles of whiskey and tequilla in case the desert heat had dried the riders' throats. In a mere few minutes it seemed that everyone in town knew of the arrival of the two riders.

Only two kinds of riders ever came to this remote place. Either men who were brave, or those who were just plain loco. As the two riders turned a wide corner the street seemed to open up to three times the span of the lanes they had been riding through. Zococa eased his pinto to a walk. His companion followed suit.

An excited crowd had gathered; a lot of men and women were engaged in frenzied gambling. The bandit held his reins loosely in his right hand as both horses drew close to a roped-off section of the street. Zococa gestured to his Apache partner. The Indian simply nodded.

A cockfight was in full heat. Feathers floated up into the dry air as the screeching of the birds almost challenged that of the people. The sand of the area called the pit was covered in the crimson proof that many cocks had already done lethal battle that day.

The two horsemen urged their mounts on.

In the majority of towns the two riders visited it was rare to see any Indians walking freely along the boardwalks, but here there were plenty. Sombreros outnumbered the smaller-brimmed Stetsons and it seemed that everyone was welcome anywhere as long as they had money to spend. Proof if any were needed that the law and civilized folks had yet to bring their rules, customs and prejudices to this place.

The largest of the saloons lured the bandit and he steered his stallion directly towards it. Tahoka followed, as he always followed, a few paces behind.

Zococa halted his stallion a few feet from the hitching rail outside a saloon with the flaking painted words BLOODY HELL on a weathered board nailed to the porch overhang.

After guiding his mount to the hitching pole, Tahoka dismounted swiftly and stood between both horses as his younger friend studied the area and the curious faces who watched him with unsmiling expressions. The Apache tapped the bandit's leg and Zococa looked down into the grim face.

'I too am a little troubled, *amigo*,' the bandit admitted. He threw his left leg over his mount's neck and slid down to stand next to his tall comrade, between the two horses. 'Just stay close to me and keep your hand on your pistol. I think many men and possibly women as well like to back-shoot here.'

Tahoka looped and then secured the reins of both horses to the rail and followed Zococa up towards the boardwalk. The bandit ducked under the crooked rail but the huge Indian simply stepped over it.

'Damn strangers,' a voice said from somewhere amid the flow of men on the boardwalk. 'I hates strangers.'

Zococa and his tall friend stopped and looked out at the people who were heading right for them. Men of every shape and size were being lured to them as if they expected another cockfight to happen, this time without roosters being involved.

Within seconds the crowd was as large as the one gathered at the cockfight down the street. Every eye watched them with burning curiosity. It did not ease the concern of the handsome bandit as he placed a hand on the swing doors and pushed his way into the saloon, with his friend guarding his back.

As both walked across the stale sawdust towards the long bar they heard the crowd follow them into the saloon. Neither man looked back, for both knew that there was always someone who was looking for any hint of weakness and fear. The long mirror behind the bar counter was amazingly clean considering the rest of the saloon's interior. It provided both men with a perfect view of what was happening behind them.

Zococa aimed his dust-caked boots at the bar and the friendly-looking man with a waxed handlebar, who was standing with a cloth in his hands.

'Howdy, strangers,' the man greeted the pair. 'Thirsty?'

'*Sí.*' Zococa answered without taking his eyes from the mirror. 'A bottle of whiskey, *señor.*'

The barkeep turned and plucked a bottle off the shelf behind him. He placed it down with two thimble glasses. 'That'll be—'

Zococa tossed a coin at the man who caught it expertly. 'I think that will cover it, *amigo*. Keep the change.'

'Wish all my customers was as easy as you two boys.' The man bit the coin, then walked to his cash drawer and dropped it in. 'Some of these varmints

77

would stab ya in the back for a glass of rye.'

'All men are not Zococa, *señor*' the bandit said.

A gasping sound went around the saloon. It was as though every man inside the Bloody Hell had inhaled at the very same time.

'I heard of you,' the barkeep said.

Zococa smiled.

Tahoka looked at the thimble glass he had been given, then turned and grabbed a beer glass from the hand of a sorrowful-looking man leaning sleepily on the bar counter. The Apache shook the beer from it, then pulled the cork of the whiskey bottle.

The man opened one eye and slurred. 'A man can git himself plugged doing things like that, redskin.'

The stone-faced Tahoka filled the glass, then turned to the objector. As the man unsteadily tried to stand he realized how big the warrior was.

'Ya lucky I'm in a good mood,' the man said.

Tahoka rested the glass down for a moment. It was long enough for him to lift the drunken man off his feet and hold him up above his head. The man screamed. Tahoka then threw the wriggling body across the bar with all his might. The man hit three others and they all tumbled across the sawdust floor before crashing into a stack of tables and chairs. Spittoons flew in every direction, throwing their contents over all who were within spitting distance. One of the dazed men on the floor went for his gun as he staggered back to his feet.

'Prepare to die, Injun,' the man howled.

The gun exploded into action. A cloud of black smoke encircled its barrel as a bullet flew across the wide room towards the two strangers in El Diablo. The heat of the bullet was felt by both men at the bar. Zococa did not flinch as his left hand went for his silver gun. He drew it in one swift action and fanned its hammer.

His bullet caught the gunman in his right shoulder. He spun on his heels before crashing back on to the three other men lying between the splintered wood of chairs and tables.

'You really are Zococa,' the barkeep gasped in awe as the bandit holstered his weapon as speedily as he had drawn it. 'Only Zococa could shoot like that.'

'*Sí, amigo.*' Zococa said, loudly enough for everyone in the Bloody Hell to hear. 'I am the great Zococa and I am going to take over this town.'

Not one man dared to argue.

'Come, my little one.' Zococa poured himself a glass of the crude whiskey and sipped at it before making his way back to the swing doors of the saloon and the blazing sunlight beyond. Tahoka followed with his glass in one hand and the bottle in the other. This time the crowd did not follow. This time they simply parted like the Red Sea upon the arrival of Moses and his followers.

The two men stood on the boardwalk side by side. The reputation of the man who favoured his left hand had reached this place long before Zococa had arrived. The cunning bandit knew that it was now up to him to exploit that reputation.

Zococa raised a finger to his chin, then glanced up at the expressionless face of his friend.

'I think we got their attention,' he whispered.

Tahoka downed the entire contents of the glass and gave out a loud belch. He then spotted the thing which was at the centre of his partner's plan. He tapped the bandit's arm and pointed with his ice-cold stare.

Zococa smiled again. This time it was broader than before.

'Ah. The bank. Soon we shall have all its blood money, Tahoka. Soon we shall have every one of these worthless creatures on our tail.'

The big Apache warrior nodded in agreement, then refilled the small glass in his friend's hand before emptying the remainder of the whiskey bottle into his far larger vessel. He tossed the bottle aside, then spoke with his fingers to the only man who could read his silent words.

Zococa downed the whiskey and placed the small thimble glass on the edge of the windowsill. He knew what his friend had asked and gave a long sigh.

'No, *amigo*. I shall not be making love to any of the

women in this town.' The bandit tightened the draw-string of his sombrero and stepped down into the street. His expression was serious as he stared down at the ground. 'I have only two females in my mind and they are with the Comancheros. Zococa will not rest until he has freed them.'

NINE

A new day had witnessed the birth of a new man. A man who had risen from the ashes of his own despair like mythical the phoenix. Marshal Hal Gunn had somehow managed to cast off the demons which had plagued him since his gruesome discovery less than thirty-six hours earlier. His mind had shattered like a cheap beer glass but when the words of the flamboyant stranger had sunk into his soul, Gunn had managed to find a way of fighting his way back. Knowing that his beloved wife and daughter were not dead had given him the strength and determination to carry on. Now he knew that there was hope. A thin sliver of hope, but that was all the star rider needed.

A mere sliver to cling on to.

He had washed the blackened reminder from his clothing and body in the river close to his burned-out homestead, and had changed into the Sunday best he always kept in his saddle-bags. Yet he was not going to church to worship, he was going on a more deadly mission. A mission which would demand every ounce of his once abundant resolve. Zococa had given him that resolve and he would not waste a solitary ounce of it. If the Comancheros wanted a fight, he would give it to them. He was no old man or small child to be frightened and then mercilessly killed. Hal Gunn was the match of all whom he had encountered over the years he had worn his star. He hit what he aimed his gun at.

Clad in his finery and with the resounding words of the young bandit who had insisted that his wife and daughter were alive, still echoing in his soul, the seasoned star rider knew that ahead of him lay far greater odds than any he had previously encountered. He would be taking on the most fearsome force of evil known in the Wild West.

The Comancheros.

Now the name filled Gunn only with hatred and the burning desire to seek retribution. He had buried any fearful concern or doubts with old Ezra and little Harry. From this moment onward he was on a crusade. A crusade to find and free his remaining family from the clutches of the two-legged vermin who had abducted them.

Gunn checked his mount as his deputy tightened his own cinch straps. Both men looked at one another briefly. Each knew he could trust the other with his life. Both had done so many times. There was an unspoken code between them. A code which for a while the marshal had forgotten, but now he remembered.

The wind swept across the flat land around them. Soon the sand blown off the prairie would cover the bloodstained ground and leave only fading memories of what had occurred here. Nature had a way of cleaning up the mess made by men.

Jones dropped his fender, held on to his saddle horn and stepped into its stirrup before hoisting himself up on top of his horse. He held on to his reins and watched Gunn carefully. He had seen the man go from solid lawman to near lunacy and now he witnessed the marshal's return to sanity and resolve.

'Ya figure on us trailing that Zococa varmint, Marshal?' Jones asked. His hands toyed nervously with his reins as the horse beneath him pawed at the ground. 'Him and that Injun seemed to know where they was heading.'

Gunn mounted. He sat and looked at the concerned features of the youngster. Then he smiled. 'Nope. Like I told ya yesterday I'm figuring on heading over to El Diablo and rustling us up a posse, boy.'

It was a troubled Jones who carefully turned his

horse. He could not hide the trepidation in his face as he eased his mount closer to the lawman he always followed. 'But them critters over in El Diablo is the most ornery folks there is, Marshal. They ain't much better than the Comancheros themselves. Some folks even say that they are in cahoots with the Comancheros. We ain't gonna find no one there willing to be sworn in and ride with us. They'll most likely shoot us dead as soon as they spots our stars.'

Marshal Gunn chewed on his lip. 'Yeah. I reckon ya could be right. Ain't bin a star rider ever gotten anything out of that cess pool except grief.'

'Ain't no law there,' Jones added. 'None at all.'

'Excepting gunlaw,' Gunn corrected. 'And we sure need us guns. We ain't in no position to be choosy.'

'We oughta ride north to Cooperville,' Jones ventured. 'We'd have us no trouble finding a hundred men there willing to be deputized.'

'Cooperville is three days' ride.' The marshal sighed as he stared out towards the ridge and the trail which was now being blown away by the prairie breeze. 'Ain't got that kinda time to waste, Toby. Three days there and three days back is the best part of a week. Who knows where Virginia and Polly could be in that time? Nope. Like it or not we gotta ride to El Diablo.'

The deputy looked at the concern on the marshal's face. He knew the older man was clutching at straws in the vain hope that they might be able to rescue his wife and daughter. It was suicidal but Jones would not openly say so. He would just follow the man he considered more like a father to him than his real one had ever been. If Gunn led him into the jaws of Hell, the loyal deputy would follow. 'Ya right, Marshal. Maybe they got themselves some religion since I was last there.'

'I surely doubt it. The last preacher who went to El Diablo met his Maker a lot sooner than he'd figured.' Gunn gathered up his reins and stared at them in his gloved hands. 'We gotta try to gather us up a posse though, Toby. We have to try and see whether there are some honest men there who'll be willing to help us. Right?'

'Right.' Jones heard himself agree. Every instinct inside the deputy wanted to argue another course of action but he was agreeing with the man he respected more than any other. 'We can sure try, I guess.'

The marshal was now thinking more clearly than he had done for the longest while. Gunn unpinned his marshal's star and poked it down into the deep pocket of his black coat. 'Ya better take that star off and hide it, son. We don't want anyone in El Diablo using it as a target.'

'If ya say so, Marshal.' Jones reluctantly removed his star and pushed it into his pants pocket. 'I surely don't like hiding my star though.'

'Me neither,' Gunn agreed.

'I'm proud of it, ya know?'

'We're still star riders, boy.' Gunn nodded firmly. 'Whatever them lowlife back-shooters think we are, just remember that we're still star riders.'

'Yep.' Jones smiled. 'We're star riders.'

Gunn tapped his spurs. Jones did the same.

Both rested horses walked slowly around the fresh graves marked by two crosses fashioned from twisted branches, then headed due west. Dust hung on the dry air as the mounts responded to the gentle encouragement of their masters. The star riders allowed their horses to find their own pace. Neither knew what lay in wait for them in El Diablo.

Whatever it was they would face it.

They were star riders.

TEN

The wide street offered little cover from either the blazing sun or the bullets both men knew could come at them from the breed of lawless creatures who occupied El Diablo. Yet defiantly Zococa walked straight down the centre of the town's main thoroughfare, holding on to the reins of his magnificent stallion. Tahoka walked his own mount a few paces behind his fearless friend and kept his drawn gun cocked and ready for action. If even the sound of a gun hammer being cocked into readiness filled his ears the huge brave would act far faster and with more lethal intent than any of the townsfolk could ever have imagined possible. The Apache knew what the bandit had planned and would back him to the hilt. The hooded eyes of the Indian narrowed as they watched Zococa stop beside the hitching rail outside a small café and loop the long leathers around it.

The bandit secured his reins in a firm knot just as the Apache brave reached the horse and its master. He tied his own reins tightly, then turned to face the men who watched their every move. In all the towns they had ever been to, the Indian had never before seen so many eyes watching them.

Zococa stepped away from his mount, lifted his leg and stepped on to the weathered boardwalk. It creaked as it took his weight. Yet the bandit did not hear the creak. His full attention was on the bank a hundred yards further along the street. Tahoka stepped up beside him and folded his arms with the Colt .45's barrel resting on his shoulder. The well polished gun caught the sunlight. Not one set of curious eyes could fail to see the weapon in the silent brave's huge hand.

Both men turned and walked along the boardwalk beneath the porch overhangs. With measured steps the two men headed straight towards the bank. Scores of people watched their every move with a curiosity that burned in their craws.

'The bank is very inviting, Tahoka,' Zococa said as they reached its front door. 'Come. We shall investigate.'

Boldly both men entered the large adobe building and felt the cooler air of the interior wash over them. The three people inside it were all dressed in white shirts with garters just above their elbows. Black visors shielded their eyes from the light of the large oil lamp hanging from a joist over the centre of the room. All sat behind a long desk with books before them. A safe almost as tall as Zococa stood behind them with its door partly closed.

The bandit noticed that the safe had a single hole in it for a key. He smiled broadly as one of the clerks cleared his throat and leaned towards him across the counter.

'Can I help ya, stranger?'

'*Sí, amigo.*' Zococa pulled a golden coin from his jacket pocket and handed it to the man. 'Can you exchange this for paper money? My friend is very hungry and I do not have any small change for the café.'

'Fifty-dollar golden eagle,' the clerk said. He bit the coin and turned to the safe. He opened the door and placed the coin in a tray with hundreds of similar ones. Then he returned to the desk, counted out fifty dollar bills and handed them to the smiling bandit. 'Anything else?'

Zococa shrugged. 'No, *señor*. Not at the moment. *Adios.*'

The two men walked out into the hot street. Zococa pushed the bills into his pocket and gave the street another quick glance.

'There is a side door which leads to the alley,' Zococa said. 'I saw two bolts. The street door has also two bolts. I do not think that this bank is very strong.'

Walking beside his friend, Tahoka watched the street and the men who still watched them. He unfolded his arms and moved his fingers quickly beneath the nose of the bandit.

'I know you could tear the side door off its hinges with your bare hands, my little one,' Zococa agreed. 'This you will do later when the sun has set.'

Both men paused when they reached the outside of the café once again. Tahoka sniffed the air filled with the aroma of cooking food and rubbed his empty stomach before pointing to his mouth.

'I know you are hungry.' Zococa took hold of the door handle and turned it. He paused briefly and looked at his companion. 'The bank, it has much money in that safe, my little hungry one.'

Tahoka gave a thoughtful nod and waited for his friend to enter the café.

'And I think that the people here will be very angry when we steal it.'

The Apache nodded again.

'But it is the only way for us to get these people to do what I want them to do. They would never will-ingly help us go into the land where the evil Comancheros hide. But when I steal their money and head on out into the desert, they will have to follow us if they want their money back. Am I not right, my little one?'

91

Unable to fend off the pangs of hunger for another second, Tahoka pushed the door open, marched into the café and sat down at the nearest table. He rubbed his stomach once more.

Zococa looked at the buxom female who stood close to a wood-fed stove. He smiled. 'The biggest steaks you have for my little friend.'

'How'd he want them cooked?' she asked politely.

'I assure you that it does not matter.' Zococa closed the door and looked out through its glass panel at the street.

If there were such things as miracles one was here in the heart of the arid desert. Beyond the enervating heat haze a sudden vision of hope appeared like a tantalizing mirage. But this was no mirage, it was real. As real as the dust-caked riders who had once again found their secret sanctuary. For miles in all directions there was nothing but mountains of white sand. Then in a deep canyon flanked by walls of solid red rock an oasis worthy of the name greeted the ruthless troop of bandits. Driving their stolen horses before them the Comancheros headed down into its vast fertile expanse.

The blazing sun rippled across a huge lake of fresh spring-water. It lay at the very centre of the quarter-mile long canyon, and was surrounded by lush vegetation. Trees of many varieties gave shade to the

Comancheros who had remained at the oasis whilst Tipah Porter had led the rest of their deadly band on their latest foray. Tents were scattered along the length of the canyon floor, with only one solidly constructed building close to the lake. The sun danced across the hefty padlock which secured its equally sturdy door. There was a good reason for this structure to be different from the rest. It was where the Comancheros housed their female captives.

The females they kept locked up here were more valuable than any of the gold the bandits had stolen over the years. The fairer the females' hair and skin, the more valuable they were. For there were still countless men of every shade who desired to own such creatures.

To own and use as they wished.

Some things were indeed more precious than gold.

As the wagon meandered behind the leader of the infamous Comancheros Tipah Porter raised an arm with a clenched fist and gave out a blood-curdling cry.

It was the hideous sound such as only the victorious could or would ever make. It was a declaration to their unseen gods that once again the cursed Comancheros had triumphed.

No army ever to ride through this territory had managed to be more successful than the one Tipah

Porter had created. But no other army had chosen to prey totally upon the innocent and vulnerable. To kill old men and young children and only take prisoners whom they knew they could sell. Porter's targets were always unprotected. It was easy for those who had no morality to defeat the meek.

Porter dropped to the ground and inhaled the scent of the lake. He looked at his followers. He removed his war bonnet and hoisted it above his head.

'Lock up these females with the others,' he ordered.

Those around him did as he said. He watched as the tethered women and girls were dragged from the back of the wagon and led towards the building in a long line. Each of them bore evidence of the blood they had shed during their vain fight against their attackers. The eyes of Virginia Gunn flashed like daggers at the men around her as she kept firm hands on her bewildered and frightened child. The defiant female kicked out with bare feet at the heavily armed men, who laughed at her and those around her. All she managed to do was impress the flamboyant figure of Tipah Porter as he surveyed their catch.

'She is like the wild mountain puma, Tipah,' one of Porter's henchmen remarked to his leader. 'I have never seen one such as that. She fights like a cat.'

Porter's eyebrows rose when he surveyed the handsome figure of Virginia Gunn as she led her terrified daughter towards their prison. The bright sun made their hair appear even more golden than he had noticed when they had captured them.

'She is mine, Pedro,' Porter vowed firmly. 'Only I shall taste her fruit. Her juices shall run down my chin like the nectar of the gods, Pedro.'

'A man could lose his eyes to a woman with fire in her belly like that, Tipah,' the bandit drooled. 'But it might be worth it.'

Tipah Porter tossed his feathered headdress aside and rested his knuckles on his hips. He had seen something which he desired. However long it might take to break her spirit and will, he would have her.

'There shall be feasting this night,' he announced loudly.

A cheer resounded amongst the Comancheros.

ELEVEN

The sky was darkening fast across the remote border town. Long black shadows were spreading through its streets like a creeping cancer. Nothing could stop them from engulfing everything in their path until the sky above was filled with a thousand stars. To some it meant another night of revelry. To a couple it meant a protective cloak. To one man it meant a chance to have his hired guns do his bidding. If El Diablo had any real leaders amid its abundance of lawless vermin it was Diamond Rufas McCloud. A man whose favourite jewels sparkled in proclamation of his unrivalled power. Stick pins and golden rings were encrusted with the ice-cold diamonds he lavished upon himself. The gambler had made a fortune since he had brought in his small troop of card-sharps, soiled doves and heavily armed protectors to the remote border town and erected his

Diamond Pin House. McCloud had arrived at virtually the same time as the infamous Comancheros had first appeared like creatures from the depths of Hell itself. Some said that it had not been a coincidence and that the gambler was in league with the infamous bandits, as well as with Satan himself.

McCloud did indeed seem to have more than his fair share of wealth. Whatever the truth, the man who was adorned in diamond pins also had more say than most of the other businessmen within the boundaries of El Diablo.

When McCloud spoke, others fearfully listened. No one in the lawless settlement had ever contradicted anything which came from the lips of the gambler. To do so was to be found dead in an alley.

From the balcony of his gambling-house the well-dressed gambler surveyed the scene below his high vantage point and brooded. The torches to the east of the town were slowly being lit as darkness rapidly swallowed El Diablo. The wide thoroughfare was still a contrast of light and dark, though. The relentless shadows snaked ever onward across the middle of the boisterous town's sand.

But the gambler had other things troubling him besides the inevitable advancement of night. McCloud was not sure what to make of the two strangers in their midst. All he knew for sure was that they might be dangerous. All strangers posed a threat to men like McCloud. For they had not been saddle broke and did not know the unspoken rules that he had established.

The gambler had heard of the bandit known as Zococa who rode with the large mute Apache. The stories he had heard were not those of a bandit like all those he had previously encountered. The stories were of a man who actually exceeded his own reputation for audacity. If Zococa was a bandit, he was unlike any other.

With the sun setting fast and the town quickly darkening, Diamond Rufas McCloud scratched a thumbnail across the tip of a match and watched as it ignited into flame. He raised the match to the end of his long black cigar and inhaled the strong smoke deeply. He kept watching the small café a hundred or so yards up the street, and the two horses tied to its hitching rail. It felt like an eternity since McCloud had seen the two men enter the eating hole.

As a trail of grey smoke trailed from his mouth the gambler heard the familiar footsteps of his trusty right-hand man Clu Parks walking to his side. Without turning his attention from where the pinto stallion and the smaller black horse were tethered, McCloud spoke.

'What ya figure that Zococa is up to, Clu?' the gambler asked.

Parks rubbed his neck. 'I ain't sure, boss. That critter is trying to git every eye on him for some reason. He bin saying he'll take over this town. He even shot one of the Bloody Hell boys. Folks said he was fast. Damn fast.'

McCloud gave a slight nod. 'Is he loco?'

'I sure reckon he must be.' Parks shrugged and also looked down the street to the café and the two horses tied to its hitching rail. 'Either that or he's playing some kinda game with us. I can't figure it none, though.'

The gambler looked up at the sky. 'No matter. It'll be dark soon.'

The shadows were now mingling into one.

'That critter went into the bank earlier,' Parks told the gambler.

'What he do?' McCloud's tone sounded concerned, for he had most of his fortune in its safe.

'Just changed a golden eagle for greenbacks.'

The gambler inhaled more smoke deep into his lungs, allowed it to linger for a few seconds, then blew it at the air. 'I've heard tales that he's a bank robber, as well as many other things. Are ya sure that all he did was get some cash?'

'Yep.'

'He must be planning something.' McCloud rubbed his thumbnail across his lips thoughtfully and then turned back to look at the café again.

'What ya want me and the boys to do about him, boss?'

'Kill him.'

Parks nodded. He had turned to leave the balcony when he felt the grip of his employer clutching at his arm. He paused and looked at the wide-eyed expression on McCloud's face. The unblinking eyes were glued to the café far along the wide street.

'What's wrong, boss?'

McCloud pointed with his cigar. 'Look.'

Parks looked. 'At what?'

'They're gone.' The gambler stammered in disbelief. 'Their horses are gone.'

Clu Parks rested both hands on the railing and squinted down to where the black shadows had enveloped the hitching pole outside the café. Both horses had indeed gone.

'I don't understand, boss. Where'd they go? I never seen either of them varmints come out of that café and take them mounts.'

'I knew it,' McCloud snarled angrily. 'He's got something planned.'

Parks had never seen his boss so troubled. 'But there's only two of them, boss. What could they do?'

'That bastard is playing with us, Clu.' McCloud flicked the ash from his cigar. 'But Diamond Rufas don't like games. He'll burn in hell if he does try anything.'

'Maybe they've just lit out,' Parks suggested. 'Maybe they bin warned about you, boss. Even Zococa must have brains enough to figure when he's taken on more than he can chew. Nobody in their right mind takes you on these parts.'

'I ain't taking no chances, Clu,' McCloud snarled as smoke drifted from his cigar and mouth. 'There's only one way to handle a critter like Zococa and that's to eliminate him.'

'Maybe he was just bluffing,' Parks reasoned. 'I figure he was just trying to ruffle a few feathers and now he's run off scared.'

'Not him. That *hombre* is up to something. Something that might cost me dear. Why'd he go into the bank? Why?' McCloud rammed his cigar into his mouth and squared up to his top gun. His eyes were narrowed as they burned into the face of the confused gunslinger. The gambler poked his finger into his henchman's chest to emphasize every following word. 'Round up the boys and tell them that if they see either of them varmints anywhere in El Diablo I want them dead. Savvy? Dead.'

'Yep, I savvy.' Parks touched the brim of his Stetson, turned and walked.

McCloud looked back down to the café. A lamp inside the small building had just been lit. Its light beamed out on to the hitching pole. 'Whatever ya up to, Zococa, its gonna cost you ya life.'

101

TWELVE

With its blazing torches perched high on its walls it still stood out like a beacon in the arid landscape, but the way station at Adobe Flats was far quieter than it had been only a few years earlier. The Overland Stagecoach Company had been going through hard times for more than a year since the railroad had expanded its routes with countless spur lines into hitherto inaccessible terrain. The once busy station was now run by a skeleton crew and saw only one stagecoach travelling in either direction each day. From a distance, though, it still looked impressive with its fortress-like walls surrounding seldom-used buildings and corrals for the teams of fresh horses.

Where once there had been ten people living and working in the way station there were now only three. Ted Smith had been the manager since the once valuable asset had been constructed out in the heart of the prairie. Now he knew that the days of the stagecoach and his job were numbered. The lean Texan had two Mexican wranglers. Between them they did all the work.

Two torches burned at either end of the long station's walls, above its open gates. There was a stagecoach due before midnight and all three men were alert to the fact that the faster they did their jobs, the faster they could finish for another twelve hours.

The way station was set exactly seven miles from El Diablo but it had been a long time since that rugged town had been on the company's itinerary. The three men inside the station were awaiting the stage headed for Cooperville. It was rare for there to be many people travelling on any of the company's night stages, and Smith knew that their job would probably only entail switching a spent team for a fresh one. He yearned for the days when each coach was full and the passengers would all eat and drink and even spend the night. It had been an interesting job then. Now boredom was the only company Smith could rely upon.

A bugle far off in the distance let out a single blast. Smith rushed to the east wall to where his own bugle was hanging on a rope and lifted the instrument to his lips. After inhaling some of the cool evening air, he blew a resounding answer. It was a ritual that harked back to the days when stations were often raided and the stagecoaches relied upon a signal that all was well and they could come in. If there was no reply the driver would know that there was trouble and divert to another route.

'The stage is coming, boys,' Smith shouted to his two men as they led out a fresh six-horse team.

The station master made his way back to the already traced horses and his small crew. He inspected the animals, then patted both his workers on their backs. He pulled his golden hunter from his vest pocket and inspected its dial by the light of a flickering torch. 'Should be here in about ten minutes or so by my reckoning.'

No sooner than the words had left his mouth than all three men heard a noise coming from the opposite gate. They turned as one man to look towards and beyond the west gate.

'What was that, Señor Ted?' Pablo Gonzales asked as he held on to the bridle of the lead horse, which was shackled in the traces.

Unsure, Smith pushed back his hat off his temple and squinted. It was dark out beyond the light of the station's torches. Whatever it was, he could not see a thing.

'Damned if I know.'

Then the answer to their question was resolved. The sound of hoofs began to echo around the walls of the station as horses beat down on the well-trodden ground leading to the gate.

'Riders,' Smith said in a low, troubled drawl. 'What would riders be doing out here at this time of night?'

It had been a long time since there had been any sort of trouble in these parts. The Apaches had long since deserted this unforgiving land and few outlaws ventured into such hazardous terrain. Yet Smith had never been complacent.

The other Mexican walked away from the team of horses and stood next to the manager.

'I hope it's not Comancheros, Señor Ted,' Ruiz Estrados muttered nervously.

Smith looked at the short, strurdy Estrados. 'What makes ya think them varmints would be in this country, Ruiz?'

'The drivers have bin telling me that the evil ones have raided many ranches around here during the last couple of weeks, *señor*,' the man answered. 'I am very scared.'

'Hell, it's more than likely just a couple of drifters,' Smith opined. 'Could be just cowboys.'

'I am still scared.'

The station master rubbed his chin. 'Go git us a few rifles from my office. Best to be safe rather than regretful.'

'*Sí, señor*,' Estrados said. He turned and ran quickly across the sandy ground to the office set amid the array of buildings.

The tall, thin Smith remained close to the team of horses as the sound of the approaching hoofs grew louder and louder and their beats echoed off the walls which surrounded them.

'I am scared as well, Señor Ted,' Pablo admitted.

'You and me both, son.' Smith winked.

'If it is trouble the shotgun guard on the stage-coach will help us when they get here, I think,' Pablo added just as Ruiz came running out of the long building with three Winchesters in his arms.

Smith inhaled deeply. 'That stage has only just come over the mesa road, Pablo. By the time it gets here. . . .'

Panting like a worn out hound, Ruiz reached his two companions and handed a rifle to each of them.

'Ya get these off the rack, Ruiz?' Smith asked.

'No, *señor*,' the young Mexican replied. 'I get them from the chest by the window.'

Ted Smith looked anxious. 'Damn it all. These rifles ain't loaded, son. The ones in the rack are loaded. These are just old carbines the company told me to get ready to be shipped back to the company for melting down.'

Each of the three cranked the rifles' handguards and looked into the magazines. Smith was right. None of them was loaded.

'I shall get the other rifles, *señor*,' Ruiz said, and

threw his Winchester to the ground.

Smith stepped forward.

'Too late, son,' the station master said. 'Look.'

Two horsemen rode through the open west gate at a slow, deliberate pace. The eyes of the three men were fixed upon them as they kept on riding towards them and the team of horses.

'Who are ya?' Smith bellowed out with the empty rifle in his hands. 'Answer me or I'll cut ya both in half.'

The horsemen stopped their mounts and sat silently watching the trio of nervous men.

'Please put the rifle down, *amigo*,' Zococa said. His left hand hovered above his holstered pistol.

'Why should I?'

'Because I will be forced to kill you if you don't.'

Smith felt ice-cold sweat run down his spine beneath his shirt. He swallowed hard. 'Who are ya?'

'They call me Zococa, *señor*.'

Both the Mexicans standing next to the team of fresh horses gasped in recognition of the name.

'Why ya here?' Smith asked.

'To steal a stagecoach, *amigo*,' the smiling bandit explained. 'Why else would I be in this place?'

Smith lowered, then dropped the empty rifle, He indicated to Pablo to do the same. Then he waited as both riders rode their mounts up to them.

'Why'd ya want to steal a damn stagecoach for,

boy?' the station master asked.

'It is a matter of life and death, *señor,*' Zococa answered.

'How come?'

'Because my little *amigo* and me have to defeat the Comancheros.' Zococa smiled.

'Are ya loco?' Smith gasped. 'Only someone plumb crazy would even think about going up against them cut-throats.'

Zococo shrugged and looked down at Smith until their eyes met. 'Maybe, *señor,* but the lives of innocent females are at stake. I have vowed to try and save them even if it costs Zococa his life.'

Then the attention of all the men inside the walls of the way station were drawn to the sound of the approaching stagecoach as it entered the last few hundred yards towards the blazing torches.

Smith rubbed his neck with his large hand. 'And ya need a stagecoach?'

'There is no time to explain why, but I need a stagecoach to achieve my plan.' The bandit was no longer smiling. There was an urgency in his handsome features.

Pablo and Ruiz moved closer to the lean Smith. He cast his attention to them.

'The great Zococa would never lie, Señor Ted,' Pablo said.

'You must trust him,' Ruiz added.

'How do I even know that this is Zococa?' Smith asked them both.

Their shaking hands pointed up at the silent Tahoka.

'He is the proof, Señor Ted,' Ruiz said.

Pablo nodded. 'The giant Apache warrior always rides with the famed one.'

Focusing on the face of the man astride the pinto stallion, Ted Smith could see that the rider was serious. He gave out a long sigh. 'It'll probably cost me my job but I'll let ya have that stage and this fresh team. But ya gotta bring it back when ya finished doing whatever it is ya gonna do. OK?'

To the sound of thundering hoofs the long stage-coach came noisily through the gate and was brought to a halt behind the three station workers. As the driver and his guard made their way down from their high perches, Zococa nodded to Ted Smith.

'Only death will stop my returning the stagecoach, *amigo*.'

THIRTEEN

There was nothing to chill the souls of men out in the barren wastelands like the sounds of coyotes baying. Some said it sounded like the crying of children. Mixed with the prairie breeze and a sky filled with stars it always managed to cut deep into the fears all men harboured in their hearts. It was an ancient noise which had gone unchanged since men first managed to walk upright and challenge the world. The howls hung on the night air like omens of doom as the two star riders reined in and inhaled the effluvia of the distant town they had yet to see.

Hal Gunn steadied his nervous mount with gloved hands as the deputy turned full circle and vainly tried to see the coyotes who mocked them.

'I'm still not sure this is a good idea, Marshal,' Jones said as he eventually stopped his horse from circling his elder. 'What if we gets ourselves plugged before Zococa shows up? We sure ain't gonna be any use to ya wife and little Polly then.'

Gunn chewed on the words. But he did not respond to them, for his attention was drawn to something his keen hearing had alerted him to out in the dunes. Even the dim starlight could not hide from his honed sense the sight of dust drifting heavenward.

The deputy stood in his stirrups and stared out to where the marshal was looking.

'What is it?'

'A stagecoach, boy,' Gunn replied almost in disbelief.

'Can't be,' Jones argued. 'There ain't no stages running anywhere close to here by my reckoning.'

Gunn nodded and then pointed. 'All the same, that is a damn stage and it's headed straight at us. Open them young eyes and look, damn it.'

Jones lowered himself down on to his saddle and gave out a surprised gasp. 'Hell. It *is* a stage. If that don't beat all and no mistake.'

The marshal gripped his leathers hard and held them to his chest as his dust-caked eyes watched the six-horse team draw closer and closer to where they held their mounts in check.

'I don't get it either, Toby. Ya right about this not being on any stage route I knows about any more, but that is a stagecoach and. . . .'

111

The deputy glanced at his superior when the older man paused. 'What's wrong?'

'He said he'd find us,' the marshal muttered.

'What?'

'Look, boy. It's Zococa,' Gunn announced.

'Huh?' Jones screwed up his eyes and squinted at the coach. The six-horse team continued kicking up dust as it ploughed on towards them. His own jaw dropped when he too recognized the driver of the vehicle smiling from beneath his wide sombrero. 'Ya right. It *is* him.'

The stagecoach slowed as its inexperienced driver hauled back on the heavy reins. It then came to a stop beside the two star riders. Dust from the hoofs and wheels drifted over the onlookers.

'Greetings, my friends.' The handsome bandit waved a hand and almost took a bow as his foot kept the brake pole firmly pressed down. 'It is good that I found you before you rode into El Diablo, for they would surely kill you.'

Gunn tapped his spurs and urged his horse to walk to just beneath the driver's perch of the stagecoach. He glanced along the vehicle and saw Tahoka seated inside. The marshal looked to the rear of the coach and saw the two horses tied to the its tailgate.

'Where'd ya get this?' Gunn asked.

'I stole it, I think.' Zococa grinned. 'I might just have borrowed it, but it's all the same. I have it.'

112

'I thought ya was trying to find my wife and daughter, not go out stealing stagecoaches,' Gunn snorted.

'Do not fret. I know where the Comancheros' camp is, *amigo*,' Zococa said. 'They cannot hide from me.'

'Then why'd ya steal a useless thing like this?' Gunn asked. 'Why ain't ya there and not here? It don't figure this none.'

'I had to steal this very pretty coach, *señor*.' The bandit shrugged as he patted the driver's seat. 'This is part of my plan. You cannot go up against so many foes without a plan.'

Gunn looked sternly up into the face which refused to stop smiling down at him. 'Plan?'

'*Sí.*'

Jones pushed his hat brim up off his brow. He was curious and it showed. 'What kinda plan ya got that needs a huge stagecoach, Zococa? I'd have thunk that something as big as this thing would kinda hamper a real smart plan. I'd have figured ya would want to sneak up on them varmints. Hell, they'll spot ya a mile off in that.'

'Exactly. I want them to see me.' Zococa nodded and waved a finger at the deputy. 'I also need this beautiful coach to put all the gold and money in, *amigo.*'

Gunn looked at Jones and then back at the bandit. 'What gold and money, boy? And what has this to do with rescuing my wife and daughter?'

Zococa looked frustrated at having to explain something which seemd totally obvious to him. 'I need the coach to put the money in that I am going to steal from the bank in El Diablo. Now do you understand?'

'What?' Gunn gasped.

'He said he's gonna rob the bank at El Diablo, Marshal,' Jones repeated.

'Exactly.' Zococa beamed.

'But what has that got to do with rescuing my wife and daughter, Zococa?' Gunn sighed. 'That's just plain robbery. How on earth is that gonna help?'

Zococa leaned over. 'I can read your mind, *amigo*. You were thinking that you could raise a posse in El Diablo. Right?'

Gunn gave a hesitant nod. 'Yep.'

The bandit waved a finger. 'Wrong. They are bad people there who would never help you. They would not help anyone, especially anyone wanting them to attack the Comancheros. This I worked out many hours ago. So I thought of a plan that would force them to attack the Comancheros without them even knowing it.'

Jones looked at the bandit. 'I get it.'

'Then ya a damn sight brighter than me, boy,' Gunn snapped.

'Don't ya see, Marshal? Zococa is gonna rob their

bank and use this stage to carry the money all the way to the Comancheros' camp. Them El Diablo varmints will follow and it'll be them that tussle with the Comancheros.'

Zococa grinned at the marshal. 'You have a very smart deputy there, *amigo*.'

'I was right?' Jones smiled in surprise.

'*Sí, amigo*. The townsfolk will be so intent on capturing Tahoka and the great Zococa and recovering their money that they will not even think about the Comancheros. The money will be my way of making the Comancheros think I wish to join them. The scum of El Diablo will blindly chase me wherever I lead them.'

'Ya think this will work?' Gunn asked.

'It has to work,' the bandit answered solemnly. 'Whilst the bandits and the citizens of El Diablo are fighting I shall rescue your wife and child.'

'But that means that you'll have to drive this stage right into the Comancheros' camp, don't it?' Hal Gunn swallowed hard. 'You'll be riding into the jaws of Hell itself, Zococa.'

'*Sí, amigo*,' Zococa agreed. 'But you and your deputy will be with me every step of the way.'

'Damn right. I'll be right there at ya side.' Gunn looked at Jones. 'I can't make ya risk ya life, son. If ya want to quit now I'll not hold it against ya.'

Jones touched his hat brim. 'I'll be there right at

ya side with my guns blazing, Marshal. I'm a star rider like you.'

'That you are, son,' Hal Gunn agreed. 'That you surely are.'

FOURTEEN

The town was like a firefly in the dark expanse of sand. The star riders flanked the stagecoach as the trusty Tahoka rode ahead of the six-horse team. A night sky without a moon was like a shield to the men who were riding with grim determination carved into every sinew of their tired souls. They each knew that they needed every scrap of luck they could find if they were to achieve their goal. There was no room for mistakes when you were taking on an entire town of merciless well-armed creatures.

The stagecoach closed in on El Diablo with the fearless bandit steering it into every shadow he could find. He had already worked out the exact route he would take through the maze of back alleys to reduce the chances of anyone witnessing the unusual sight of a stage inside the lawless boundaries of the remote town. The pair of star riders had flanked the vehicle for nearly an hour before it reached the outskirts El Dorado. Then, as instructed, the lawmen drew leather and halted their progress as the stagecoach rolled on, led by the eagle-eyed Apache warrior.

With the swollen saddle-bag that Tahoka had provided them with, Hal Gunn and Toby Jones steered their mounts to the cover of a ruined adobe building close to one of the town's many wells. A tall, frail, wooden structure stood near to the well. Their noses told them that this was the livery stables. Gunn could tell that there was someone inside by the light which snaked out of the gaps between its weathered wall-boards. The star riders dismounted and tethered their animals to a fence pole. Then the marshal touched his lips and nodded to his deputy. Jones knelt down, took the saddle-bags from the marshal and then watched as Gunn made his way silently towards the livery.

The sound and aroma of horses greeted Gunn as he reached the wide-open doors of the livery. He drew his .45, pressed his face up against the boards and peered in. A man built like a bull was sitting close to a forge. His snores filled the vast interior of the building. Gunn narrowed his eyes and then studied the horses in their stalls. There had to be more than forty of them. Saddles and bridles of every kind were balanced on each stall wall in readiness. The star rider knew that it would not take long for those horses to be saddled and used to pursue them. He had to buy Zococa and the rest of them some time. Enough time for the heavily laden stagecoach to reach the Comancheros' encampment before any of El Diablo's townsfolk caught up with them.

How much time?

There was no way of knowing but Gunn had to try and purchase them at least an hour. More would be better. Saddle horses could easily catch up with a stagecoach weighed down with gold, he thought. But if the bridles of every saddle were cut? A smile etched its way across his face.

That was it. It would take at least an hour for the drunken sots to repair bridles with their leathers cut. That would buy them time. That would ensure they reached the desert before their pursuers.

The marshal walked into the livery as silently as a puma stalking its prey. He turned the .45 around in his gloved hand until he was holding on to the barrel. He approached the burly dozing man and raised his arm.

He brought the six-shooter down hard. A sickening sound echoed round the stables. The man buckled and toppled forward, but he was not out. His gleaming arms reached out and grabbed hold of Gunn's legs. The marshal was stunned as he felt himself being hauled down into the sand. Blood poured from the gash across the top of the stableman's head, but he clung on and started to growl.

The pair wrestled on the sand. Blood flooded over Gunn as he felt the sheer weight of the man crawl up him until the muscular fingers were at his throat. He tried to escape but, even stunned, the man was as powerful as his size implied. Gunn used his boots to try and force himself free but the grunting man clung on.

The fingers started to squeeze at Gunn's throat.

Tighter and tighter they drew, until the star rider thought his eyes were going to pop out of his skull. He was no match for this creature. Then as he stared up into the twisted face above his own he heard another noise. It was Jones. The deputy had smashed his own six-shooter down on the head of the livery-man.

The man slumped like a dead bull. Using all his strength Jones hauled the unconscious man off the marshal and helped Gunn back to his feet.

'T-thanks, son,' Gunn croaked, rubbing his bruised throat.

Jones smiled and looked around. 'What ya reckoning on doing in here, Marshal?'

The exhausted marshal staggered to a tool box and found two well-honed knives. He handed one to his deputy. 'Cut the bridles up, Toby.'

The younger star rider grinned. 'That'll sure slow the bastards up and no mistake.'

The alley was shrouded in darkness as the team of six horses came to a stop just next to the side door of the bank. Tahoka had already dismounted from his black gelding and knotted his reins to the tailgate next to the pinto stallion. He walked silently round the vehicle and stared down into the main street where, the previous day, they had witnessed the cockfight. A scattering of street lanterns lit up the still busy street. The sound of tinny pianos from saloons drifted on the night air up into the narrow alley as Zococa clambered down to the dusty ground.

The Indian was holding on to his gun as his hooded eyes kept watch on the street. Various people were walking past from one den of iniquity to the next.

So far they had been lucky and no one had noticed their return to El Diablo, but both realized that that could change in a mere heartbeat.

Zococa was about to speak when he heard something coming along the alley behind them. It was people talking as they drew closer. Tahoka moved to the lead horses and stood between them. The bandit slid beneath the belly of the stagecoach and squinted hard into the darkness. Then he saw three sets of legs. Two sets were in pants and the third naked as they protruded from a lot of petticoats.

Two men had managed to lure one of the soiled doves from either a saloon or one of the numerous brothels. She swayed between them as they led her into the darkest part of the long winding alley. Zococa emerged from beneath the stagecoach just as all three reached the vehicle.

The men had a bottle of whiskey and were allowing the female to suck expertly on its neck. She was giggling as her companions kept her from falling on to her face.

All three abruptly stopped when they realized that they were not alone in the alley.

'I am very afraid that you boys are going to have the headache,' Zococa announced as both men focused on the bandit standing a mere yard in front of them.

'What the hell?' one of the men stammered, and his friend dropped his half-consumed bottle.

'Hey. Ain't that a stage?' the female slurred, pointing a long thin finger as whiskey dripped from her chin on to her swollen bosom. 'What's going on here?'

Zococa reached out and took the female's hands. At exactly the same moment Tahoka appeared behind the men and slammed their heads together.

Both dropped to the ground.

'Allow me, my pretty one.' The bandit stooped, plucked the bottle off the sand and handed it to the female. She giggled, pushed its neck back into her mouth and began sucking again as she continued on her way.

Zococa leaned over, grabbed the collar of one of the men and dragged his limp body into the shadows. The Apache brave did the same with the other man.

'We must act swiftly, my little one,' Zococa said urgently.

Tahoka gave a firm nod.

At the other end of town Gunn unbuckled the saddle-bag satchels and went ashen faced as his gloved hands pulled out its lethal contents. A dozen sticks of dynamite with short minute-fuses filled his hands as he rested beside the silent deputy.

'Sweet Mary,' the marshal gasped as he carefully placed the explosives down on the sandy ground. 'That young bandit thinks of everything, boy.'

Jones tentatively touched the sticks and exhaled loudly. 'I ain't never played around with these things before, Marshal.'

Gunn glanced at his younger partner. 'Me neither.'

'What he tell us to do again?' Jones asked, even though he had heard Zococa's instructions just as clearly as Gunn had.

'We wait for ten minutes, then we drop one of

these things into the well. When it explodes we start hurling the things at anyone loco enough to be curious,' the marshal explained.

'Ten minutes,' Jones repeated.

Gunn pulled out his watch from his vest pocket and flicked open its golden lid. He turned the dial until the light of countless stars illuminated the hands of his timepiece. It was nearly one in the morning. 'Ten minutes ought to give them enough time to break into the bank and fill the belly of that coach with all its money and gold.'

'According to Zococa,' the deputy added.

'Yeah.' Gunn closed the watch and returned it to his pocket. Then he dug out a box of matches. He shook them as though to convince himself that he had plenty.

Jones leaned around the corner of the broken wall and looked down along the wide main street. There was still plenty of activity going on close to the large gambling-hall and a few saloons.

'The place is still pretty busy considering the time,' he remarked. 'Reckon the folks around here don't hanker to taking it easy like most critters.'

Gunn also gave the town a long look. 'That's what's troubling me, boy. There's still too many folks wide awake.'

'And everyone of them is armed, I'll wager.'

'Yep,' the marshal agreed.

124

*

The side door of the bank might have been locked and bolted but it offered little resistance to the powerful hands of the big Apache brave. Tahoka had torn it from its hinges in one swift movement. A moment later the bandit was racing into the bank to the large safe that stood against the back wall. No locksmith could have equalled the speed with which Zococa picked the safe's lock and opened its door.

The two men worked fast to remove everything from inside the safe's interior and load it into the stagecoach. Nothing but dust remained in the safe as Tahoka closed the coach door and watched Zococa climb back up to the driver's seat. Tahoka released his horse's reins from the tailgate and threw himself up on top of the sturdy animal as the bandit carefully turned the six-horse team away from the rear of the bank.

'Any moment now, my little one.' Zococa grinned as he held firmly on to the hefty reins.

Then it happened.

A series of mighty explosions from the other end of El Diablo erupted as Gunn and Jones followed their instructions. Blazing plumes of fiery light went up into the night sky, just as Zococa had wanted.

Zococa slapped his reins down across the backs of the six-horse team. The stagecoach came hurtling out of the alley into the main street. The bandit dragged the reins hard to his left and yelled out at the top of his voice as Tahoka fired his gun up into the air.

A few seconds later the startled townspeople came tumbling out from their houses, the gambling-halls and saloons, to see what had happened. Then yet another explosion rocked the town. Stunned men and women watched as the stagecoach thundered away.

Diamond Rufas McCloud had rushed out into the street along with his patrons and henchmen. His head turned one way and then the other as his attention was torn between the explosions and the gunfire. Then he saw the two star riders as their horses galloped after the fleeing stage.

'What's going on?' McCloud screamed out in frustration.

Clu Parks appeared from the other side of the street with a look of sheer confusion written all over his face.

'They robbed the bank, boss,' Parks managed to say.

'What?' the gambler yelled.

'Zococa and that redskin done robbed the bank,' Parks repeated. 'They cleaned it out. Took everything. That's them on that stagecoach.'

Every man standing in the street suddenly realized

the gravity of the gunslinger's words. They all looked to McCloud for guidance.

'What we gonna do?' they all seemed to ask at the same moment. 'What we gonna do?'

McCloud felt his fists clench.

'What ya waiting for? Get down to the livery and saddle up as many horses as you can find, the gambler bellowed out to all of the men who were gathered in the street. 'Them varmints have stolen all our money.'

Parks looked at the stupefied faces. 'Ya heard Diamond Rufas. Get going before them thieves ride down into Mexico.'

Like a plague of locusts men swarmed down the wide street towards the livery stables.

'I'll teach that Zococa he can't rob Diamond Rufas and live to tell the tale, Clu,' McCloud vowed. 'He'll be hanging from a tree before sunup.'

FIFTEEN

The sun had spread out across the barren wastes like a tidal wave as the bandit pulled back on the reins and pushed the brake pole down. The stagecoach rolled to a halt as its trio of outriders drew rein around the dust-caked vehicle. Zococa turned on his high seat and looked back across the vast sea of dunes behind them. The hoof tracks and deep grooves left by the stagecoach team and wheels were the only marks on the otherwise virginal sand. Hal Gunn held his horse in check and looked up into the face of the exhausted bandit.

'Ya lost, ain't ya?' Gunn growled.

'Have you no faith in me, *amigo*?' Zococa smiled and then looked at Tahoka, who was studying the land behind them from atop his lathered-up gelding.

'There ain't nothing out there except more sand, boy.' The marshal pointed a finger. 'Ya said ya knew where that Comencheros camp is situated, but how can ya?'

Jones shook his head. 'I'm tuckered out, Marshal.'

'Ya ain't on ya lonesome, son,' Gunn said with a sigh.

Tahoka rode to just beneath the driver's seat of the stage and gestured frantically with his hands to his companion. The bandit nodded and showed the Apache the palm of his hand.

'Easy, my little rhinoceros. I can hear them as well.'

'Hear them?' Gunn echoed the bandit's words and a grim expression filled his face. He looked back at the mountainous dunes they had negotiated through the night and felt his heart quicken its pace. 'Ya mean them El Diablo varmints are so close to us that ya can actually hear them?'

'*Sí, amigo,*' Zococa answered. He turned to give his attention again to the team of fatigued horses. 'They are probably less than a mile behind us, I think.'

'Hell, that's close to Winchester range,' Jones quipped.

Gunn knew that even a blind man could have followed the trail they had left in the otherwise smooth desert sand. He rubbed his neck and closed the distance between the coach and his mount. He placed a hand on the brake pole, upon which Zococa still had his boot resting.

'Are ya sure ya know where them heathens are, boy?' There was concern in the tone of the star rider. It drew the eyes of the young bandit. 'I don't see nothing out there. How can ya be so certain we're headed the right way?'

'You have eyes but they do not reveal the truth to you, my friend,' Zococa said quietly. He aimed a finger at the horizon where the heat of the new day was starting to cause a shimmering haze to rise from the white dunes. 'Look and see. Look.'

Gunn released his hold on the brake pole, gripped his reins tightly and turned. His eyes narrowed as they vainly searched the line between the sand and the blue sky.

'I don't see nothing except a whirlpool of heat,' the marshal admitted. 'What can you see that I can't, boy?'

The bandit shook his head. 'You look for a camp, *amigo*. You look for bandits. You cannot see either from here but you can see something.'

'Stop talking in riddles,' Gunn growled.

'No one can hide in the desert.' Zococa lifted the reins in his hands. 'Not from the hungry buzzards who want to feast on their remains, *señor*. The birds will always betray you.'

'Buzzards?' The marshal swung back around and looked at the blue cloudless sky. A handful of black-winged buzzards were circling directly ahead of them. 'Damn it all. I see them, boy. Is that where the Comancheros' camp is?'

Zococa grinned broadly. '*Sí*. The camp is right below those buzzards.'

'I'd never have thought of that.' The star rider gave a sigh.

Zococa suddenly became serious. 'Listen. Now we have to ride into the most dangerous place. You and your young *amigo* must remember that from now on you are members of my gang. You have to become liars, so that Tipah Porter believes that you are also bandits. Otherwise he will kill you both.'

'Tipah Porter?' The marshal repeated the name. 'Who's that, Zococa?'

'He is the leader of the Comancheros,' the bandit replied. 'It is he who has the power of life and death in that camp. To live you must let me do all the talking, for otherwise he will surely kill you both.'

Gunn looked at Zococa. 'What about you and Tahoka?'

'He knows my little one and myself are bandits but he does not know you.' Zococa looked worried. 'Tipah Porter is very cruel but he is also very dangerous and very clever. If he is not convinced that you are bandits you and your deputy will die.'

'Tell me, boy,' Gunn asked the bandit, 'do ya really think that my wife and daughter are still alive?'

'It is the only thing I know for certain, *amigo*.'

Suddenly the sound of gunfire erupted behind them. All four men glanced back and saw the dark images of riders coming over the highest of the dunes. Gunsmoke blackened the air as McCloud and his followers began to unload their weaponry at the men who had stolen their money.

As bullets fell short and cut up the sand ten yards behind them Zococa released the brake pole and whipped the backs of his wearied team. The horses responded. The stagecoach began to roll again, flanked by its three outriders.

The chase had resumed.

SIXTEEN

McCloud and the forty or more men he had managed to gather together were closing in fast on the stagecoach and its three guards. Their guns were spewing out lead with every stride of their galloping mounts and each shot was getting closer to their targets. Every passing second the riders from El Diablo were closing in on their prey.

Zococa cracked the tails of his long reins across the backs of the thundering team as he steered the long vehicle towards the place which, he knew, harboured the Comancheros and their camp.

The bandit knew that it was now only a matter of time before their pursuers caught up with them. Time was running out and the exhausted six-horse team was slowing. The bullets were now getting closer.

Hal Gunn rode up to the side of the driver's high

perch and looked at the grim determination in the bandit's face. He kept on spurring his mount and looking behind them.

Jones and Tahoka were right behind the tailgate of the stagecoach and eating the dust kicked up off its wheels. Then, just as the big Indian looked back, a shot came so close that the Apache brave felt its heat. A split second later he saw Jones's mount crash into the sand and send the deputy cartwheeling. With no thought for his own safety, Tahoka dragged his own reins up and stopped his horse in its tracks. He turned the animal hard around and rode to where Jones was scrambling to his feet. The powerful Indian balanced himself in his saddle and leaned down. He grabbed the younger man by the arm and hauled him up on to the back of his own horse.

Shots flew around them as Tahoka whipped his mount's shoulders with his reins. Somehow the gelding managed to respond and was soon gaining on the fleeing stagecoach once more.

Gunn slowed his own horse when he had seen his deputy's mount shot from under him. The marshal hauled his rifle from under his saddle, cranked its mechanism and fired at the horsemen. He watched as two of his shots plucked men from their saddles. As Tahoka rode past the star rider Gunn swung his own horse around and raced after them. The marshal managed to catch up to Zococa. He screamed out to him.

'Are we gonna make it, boy?' Gunn yelled.

Zococa did not know the answer.

As the thunderous sound of gunfire came ever closer to the secret camp of the Comancheros the thirty or so heavily armed outlaws responded quickly. Even though the day was still young, they were as always ready for action. Every one of the hardened bandits had always known that one day their hideout might be attacked. That time had arrived with the lengthening rays of the rising sun.

Entirely undaunted by the sound of blazing guns which rang out from the desert, Tipah Porter strode through the ranks of his men like a wrangler guiding his herd towards the narrow entrance to their encampment. Orders spewed from his lips. He briskly climbed up the rockface and stood next to one of his sentries on a small ledge. The Mexican guard pointed the barrel of his rifle out to where the air was darkening as the forty or more horsemen repeatedly fired their weaponry at the fleeing stage-coach and its outriders.

'Who is that?' Porter mumbled, dragging the binoculars from the neck of the stunned sentry. 'Give me them spy glasses, Lopez. I wanna see who that is.'

The leader of the Comancheros raised the binoculars and adjusted its focus until he could see the face of the stagecoach driver clearly. Porter then

135

moved position and focused on the forty or more riders who were in pursuit and firing their guns.

'Who is it, Tipah?' the sentry asked as his glasses were thrust back into his hands.

'It is my old *amigo* Zococa and his tame Apache,' Porter answered. He waved down to the Comancheros below him. 'Let the coach and its riders through but stop that army of *hombres* who are trying to kill them.'

The Comancheros moved to the very edge of the oasis with their rifles primed in readiness as the sweat-soaked team of horses pulled the stagecoach over a rise of sand and brought it down into the fertile heart of Porter's encampment. The two horses carrying their three burdens followed at breakneck pace.

Porter stared out into the rising heat haze at the horsemen who refused to quit. To his utter amazement they continued to keep on coming.

'Fire!' he yelled out. No thunderclap could have matched the ear-splitting sound of the rifles and six-shooters as they fired their lethal lead out at the approaching riders.

Hauling the hefty reins back and pressing the brake pole down with his boot Zococa managed to bring the long vehicle to a stop. Clouds of dust floated over the area as his keen eyes spied the only structure in the camp to be locked.

He knew why.

Regaining his wind the bandit looked all around through dust-filled eyes. Then he saw the familiar figure of Tipah Porter clambering down from the rockface as the deafening battle continued behind him. Gunn steadied his mount and watched the flamboyant Zococa intently. Tahoka helped the deputy to the ground, then dropped down beside him.

'Remember, my friends, that only Zococa speaks,' the bandit whispered to his three followers before turning to face the most dangerous man in the territory.

With the battle growing even more intense, Zococa wrapped his reins around the brake pole, then stood in the driver's box and faced Porter. His smile greeted the broadshouldered Porter as he reached level ground.

'So why is Zococa bringing strangers into the camp of the Comancheros?' Porter pointed with his left hand at the two star riders. His right hand hovered only inches above his gun grip. 'Do you not recall that I once told you that I do not want strangers knowing of my stronghold? Many men have died for not heeding the words of Tipah Porter. Why should I spare you?'

Zococa shrugged. 'These are my men, Tipah. Tahoka is very big but to rob banks it is much safer to have extra guns. Without my extra gunmen we should not have managed to escape from El Diablo.'

Tipah Porter said nothing as the handsome bandit clambered down to the ground and stood before him. His eyes fleetingly glanced at Gunn and Jones, then his gaze returned to the still-smiling face of Zococa. 'Why do they not look like bandits, my friend?'

'This is an advantage.' Zococa gestured to each star rider in turn. 'One looks like a preacher and the other like a choirboy. Who would ever suspect such innocents were in fact deadly bank robbers?'

Porter roared with laughter. He slapped Zococa on the shoulder, then turned to where the battle was still raging at the mouth of the gulch. 'I should kill ya but maybe not just yet.'

Zococa knew that even in the desert a man could find very thin ice to walk upon. He was on very fragile ground. 'I am grateful to you, Tipah. When I die I wish it to be in the arms of a beautiful girl.'

Porter's eyes locked on those of the younger man. 'Why have you led so many fools to my hideout, Zococa?'

'They used to own this.' Zococa walked to the door of the stagecoach and opened it to reveal its contents. The bags of paper money were piled high but it was the gold bars and coins, catching the rays of the rising sun, that impressed Porter the most. He nodded.

'You were wise not to come here empty-handed, Zococa.'

The bandit gave out a gentle sigh. 'This is for you and your men, Tipah. All we wish in return is to join forces with you.'

Tipah Porter reached in and lifted a handful of the golden coins. He inhaled their aroma. 'The sweet smell of El Dorado is always a welcome scent, Zococa. Of course ya can join us. But because ya have ensured that many of my men will either die or be wounded this day, this will be recompense for your stupidity.'

Zococa signalled to Tahoka with his hands.

As fast as a sidewinder striking at its prey, Porter dropped the coins and grabbed hold of Zococa's shoulder. He dragged the bandit to him and again stared into his eyes.

'I know of ya secret language to that silent Apache,' Porter told him. 'What did ya say to him? Tell me.'

'I told my little one to get his rifle for we shall join your men and fight those who have foolishly followed us, Tipah.' Zococa lied. 'Nothing more.'

Porter released his grip. 'Remember, handsome one. If I even suspect ya lying to me I will kill ya all with a swiftness no other can equal. Savvy?'

Zococa nodded. 'You can trust me and my men. This I vow.'

The leader of the Comancheros turned to where the shooting was getting even more furious. He could already see that he had lost five of his men to the bullets of those who defiantly refused to run away. His brow wrinkled as he drew both his Colts and cocked their hammers.

'Come, Zococa. You and ya tiny army will now have to prove ya worth. We must kill every one of those who ya led to this secret place. Not one of them must be allowed to live or escape our wrath. No others must ever venture into my land.'

Zococa turned to the three men he had brought into the camp with him. 'You heard Tipah. Come. We have to kill the vermin who followed us to the Comancheros' stronghold.'

The four men trailed Porter towards the fighting.

Through a six-inch-square hole in the wooden structure's padlocked door, Virginia Gunn had been watching. As the swirling dust thinned she saw her husband's horse. Hal was here, her mind told her. He was here. But where? No matter how hard she pressed her face against the small hole she was unable to see anything but the stagecoach and the familiar horse.

They were less than thirty steps from her prison. It might as well have been a thousand miles. Tears rolled down her cheeks and she felt herself dragged away by other women even more desperate than she was herself. As Virginia Gunn fell to her knees in the darkness of the structure's interior she felt the small arms of her daughter comforting her.

There was no hiding-place at the edge of the oasis. Bodies with fatal wounds were flying backwards on all sides as Tipah Porter raced with his guns held at hip level. He started firing as soon as he caught a glimpse of the men who had dared attack his stronghold. McCloud was lying behind the body of his wounded horse as were half his men. Some of the townspeople had survived the initial volley from the Comancheros but they were becoming fewer with every blast from the bandits' rifles. Only the wounded horses gave any of them any hope of cover in the barren desert.

The thought of losing every cent kept the men of El Diablo fighting and crawling forward. Men were being cut down on all sides but the gambler was undaunted. McCloud searched the bloody sand which surrounded him for the guns of the already dead or wounded. He rammed two discarded .45s into his gunbelt and then snatched a rifle from the hands of a headless body lying close to him.

From the cover his horse gave him McCloud swung on his knees and looked around the desert sand. He tried to calculate how many of those who had followed him to this satanic place were still actually alive. He saw at least twenty.

'Come on, men,' he yelled out at them. 'Let's show

the bastards we ain't licked yet.'

For no reason which made any sense to any of them the men mustered up their weaponry, ignored their wounds and rose to their feet. They charged through the choking clouds of gunsmoke at their unseen enemies.

The Comancheros had now lost half their number and were retreating backwards into the heart of the oasis. With bullets raining in on them, Porter was stunned by the sight of the men who were now charging, on foot, his own dwindling force. The leader of the bandits waved Zococa and his three companions back.

'Damn it all. I should never have sent Jardine and Red Sky south with them steers,' Porter cursed as he too found himself forced back by a volley of bullets. He now deeply regretted having his own army reduced by half.

Zococa leapt down from the rocks and pushed Gunn and Jones behind a large boulder. 'Soon we shall be able to free your loved ones, *amigo*.'

'We oughta be killing these outlaws, Zococa,' Gunn said. 'Not pussy-footin' around like this.'

Zococa stared at the star rider hard and true. 'Not yet. To do so now would be to have Tipah Porter have all his remaining bandits turn their guns on you. Think of your wife and your child, *amigo*. They do not want you dead.'

142

Reluctantly the marshal nodded. 'OK. OK.'

Zococa, Gunn and Jones ran down through the gunsmoke after the fleeing bandits.

Tipah Porter guided his dozen or so men down into the very heart of the gulch to regroup. The air was already putrid with the burning residue of a thousand discharged shots. Black smoke lingered a few feet above the ground across the entire width of the gulch as Porter and his followers took cover.

Diamond Rufas McCloud was not finished yet. He and his men came over the sandy rim which marked the entrance to the fertile gulch with their weapons still blazing. White-hot flashes of lethal lead cut through the air in both directions as the deafening blasts echoed around the once safe haven. Men on both sides were now dropping like leaves from trees in the fall.

Zococa looked to Gunn and the deputy. 'This is not good, *amigos,*' He murmured before leaping down into the belly of the gulch amid the crossfire.

The lawmen were now trapped between two opposing forces. Just as the star riders found cover in the rocks a volley of hot lead blasted the rocks around them into a thousand fragments. Burning debris showered over them.

Toby Jones felt as though red-hot branding-irons had been shoved into his eyes. He screamed and grabbed at his face. His boots lost their grip on the crumbling rockface. He slid down the embankment helplessly.

Gunn was about to follow his deputy when another score of shots pinned him down. He clutched on to his .45 and looked down to where Jones lay. The deputy was motionless.

The star rider then saw Zococa moving through the tall grass at the very foot of the wall of rocks beneath him. The gambler had led his men to within fifty yards of where Porter and his men were hiding. Gunn studied the area all around. It was littered with bloody bodies either dead or dying.

With bullets seeking him out from both sides and coming closer with every passing moment Hal Gunn threw himself off the ledge.

He seemed to be falling downwards for ever. Yet even on his descent the bullets kept on seeking him.

Then his boots slammed on to the deep sand at the foot of the rocks. The marshal felt as though every bone in his body had suddenly been crushed. He rolled over, winded, and lay there listening to the chilling sounds of bullets as they continued ripping through the air.

Then only the cries of the wounded filled Gunn's ears. He forced himself on to his side. The fight had stopped, he told himself.

But who were the victors?

Defying his own agony he crawled to where he had last seen his deputy. He pushed the long grass down in front of him, then he saw Jones. The youngster had not moved since hitting the ground. The marshal clawed at the ground and reached his loyal deputy.

He carefully turned the young star rider over and patted his cheek. 'Toby?'

Jones's eyes flickered. They reluctantly opened and stared in dazed confusion at the marshal. 'W-what?'

'Ya ain't dead, son.' Gunn sighed thankfully.

'Sure feels like I am.'

'Easy.' Gunn checked the deputy's legs and arms. 'I reckon there ain't nothing broken.'

Jones jumped up. 'Where's Zococa? We gotta find him and Tahoka.'

Hal Gunn knew the deputy was right. They had to find both of them if they were to achieve their goal. With guns drawn both of the star riders began to crawl back along the gulch to where they had left the stagecoach and their mounts.

Zococa had paused when the gunplay had eventually stopped. The bandit was already close to the wooden structure where he knew the Comancheros kept their female captives. He drew his silver pistol and cocked its hammer as he moved from behind a line of trees to where he had seen Porter and the last

145

of his men take cover. The bandit had not even broken cover when he heard the sound of dried twigs snapping beneath the heels of a heavy boot.

'Don't even blink, Zococa.'

The voice was unfamiliar to the bandit. Zococa allowed his pistol to fall from his hand on to the ground at his feet. He then turned to look to where the voice had come from. Although Zococa did not know it, he was face to face with Diamond Rufas McCloud. The gambler looked as though every ounce of colour had been drained from his face as he waved the long-barrelled rifle under the nose of the famed bandit.

'Ya gonna pay for what you done. Pay with your worthless hide,' McCloud snarled.

'Who are you, *señor*?' Zococa enquired.

'I'm the man that's gonna kill ya,' McCloud replied. He walked slowly forward until they were face to face. 'Ya robbed my bank and led us into a trap. Every one of my men is dead, boy. Dead.'

Zococa swallowed hard. He could see the blood-stains down the man's fancy pants. A lot more blood was flowing unchecked from a hole in the gambler's belly. 'I would like to know who is going to kill Zococa, *señor*. What is your name?'

'McCloud. Diamond Rufas McCloud,' The gambler spat out his name. Then he cranked the Winchester's hand guard in one practised action.

'Now say ya prayers.'

Suddenly the sound of a gun being fired echoed all around the area as Hal Gunn fanned his .45's hammer. The star rider watched as the gambler was lifted off his feet and thrown like a rag doll across the clearing until he smashed into the ground. A trail of gore marked his flight.

'Many thanks, *amigo*,' Zococa said as Tahoka emerged from the brush and gestured to his partner frenziedly.

Both Gunn and Jones looked at the bandit. 'What's Tahoka saying?'

A grim expression wiped the smile from Zococa's face. He scooped up his pistol and moved to where the huge Apache was pointing.

'What he telling ya, boy?' Gunn asked again. This time louder than before.

'We have trouble, *amigo*. Much trouble,' Zococa said. He turned on his heels and quickly followed Tahoka into the dense undergrowth. All four men were running. Only two knew why.

A few minutes later they appeared near by the stagecoach. Five dead Comancheros lay scattered in pools of blood on the ground close to the team of horses. Zococa looked at their three saddle horses, which remained secured to the stagecoach.

Acrid gunsmoke still trailed from the hot barrels of the rifles in the dead bodies' hands. Zococa

147

grabbed hold of the Apache warrior and stopped his progress just as the star riders caught up with them.

'Easy, little one. Caution will buy us many more days.' The bandit used his keen senses as he studied everything around the area dominated by tents.

As all four men walked between the trees towards the place where they knew Porter had imprisoned his captives, Gunn shook the spent brass casings from his smoking .45 and started to reload his weapon. 'What's got ya so all fired up, Zococa? By my reckoning each side wiped the other out.'

'I am afraid that the evil Tipah Porter has been here before us, *amigo*.' Zococa said in a low, solemn tone. 'Tahoka tells me he has already taken his most prized captives.'

Gunn rammed his Colt into its holster. 'My Virginia and Polly, ya mean?'

Zococa nodded.

'Taken where?' Gunn urged.

'To where the Comancheros keep all their horses, *amigo*.'

Jones rubbed the blood from his face. 'There must be a hundred or more mustangs down at the far end of the lake, Marshal. I could see them when I was up on that ridge.'

Tahoka pointed to the door of the wooden structure where Porter had kept his captives. Its door was wide open and its padlocked chain lay on the sand.

148

The sounds of sobbing females came from within its dark interior.

Gunn frantically ran to the building and looked inside. There were females in there but not the precious two he sought. He looked back and was about to speak when he noticed Zococa running to the tailgate of the stagecoach. Gunn observed the young bandit as he leapt on the saddle of his tall stallion. The star rider blinked hard and watched Zococa pull his reins free and spur the pinto into action.

With its master hanging on the mighty black-and-white animal thundered away towards the end of the long gulch and the place where the Comancheros kept their horseflesh.

Gunn moved to his deputy's side. 'What in tarnation is that young 'un doing, Toby?'

'I'll bet ya that Zococa's gone to take on that Porter varmint on his lonesome,' Jones said fearfully. '*I* sure wouldn't wanna tangle with him alone.'

Hearing these words Tahoka drew his gun and rushed to his black gelding tied to the six-horse team's traces. He swung up on to the animal's back and hauled his reins free before gathering them up in his large hands. He used the long leathers to whip his mount into life. The Apache frantically galloped after his partner through the undergrowth down alongside the lake. All the warrior could think of was catching up to his comrade before Zococa forgot his own advice and threw caution to the wind.

Dust from the horses' hoofs swirled around the two star riders. Hal Gunn pointed to the building where the frightened females were huddled. 'You go and help them womenfolk, son. They surely needs help.'

'What you gonna do, Marshal?' Jones croaked.

But Hal Gunn did not answer. He had already pulled his tethers free of the stagecoach wheel, stepped into his stirrup and mounted his horse. He spurred and rode through the dust in pursuit of their two companions.

As the star rider rode into the dense brush beside the shimmering lake he prayed as no man had ever prayed before.

The young horseman had never before ridden at such speed. His stallion crashed everything in its path aside as Zococa stood in his stirrups and urged the powerful pinto on. The animal needed little encouragement as it leapt everything in its path and closed in on the fleeing Comanchero and his two prisoners. As the horse obeyed its master's every command Zococa began to catch taunting glimpses of them through the trees. The sun reflected off the expanse of water to his side, temporarily blinding him to what lay ahead.

Then as the young horseman ducked under a low-hanging branch and his mount charged down a wall of bushes, Zococa saw the two golden-haired females clearly. But what he did not see was the rifle in the hands of the notorious Porter. A shot carved its way across the clearing and hit the bandit's right shoulder like the kick of a mule.

The stallion stopped as Zococa rocked on his saddle but refused to fall.

The bright morning sunshine filled the far end of the long gulch where it turned into a box canyon. Hundreds of horses were there. Most were stolen but at least fifty were the Comancheros' saddle mounts. All were kept corralled by crude fence-poles which spanned the width of the canyon from high wall to high wall.

Smoke trailed out from the end of the rifle barrel. It twisted and curled out and lingered over the two heads of golden hair. Mother and child had been thrown down into the dirt next to a rugged wall of sand-coloured rock. Fear kept them both there as their captor stepped away from the trio of horses that Porter had just saddled.

Zococa held on to his reins as blood ran from his sleeve over his right wrist and hand. He had never felt such pain before. It was alien to him but he refused to turn back now.

Not with the sight of Gunn's family in his burning eyes.

151

Tipah Porter expelled the spent casing from his rifle and stepped forward until his shadow covered both Virginia and Polly.

'Ya thought I was fooled didn't ya, Zococa?' Porter said loudly. 'But I knew ya was lying through them white pearly teeth of yours all the time.'

Fighting his own agony Zococa gritted his teeth and slowly nodded as he replied, 'Then why did you not kill us when we arrived, Tipah?'

'I needed ya firepower. Nothing else,' Porter answered. He gave the two golden-haired females a darting glance before focusing his eyes on his wounded adversary. 'I had me a gut feeling it was really these handsome critters that had brought ya here.'

'Tipah Porter has lost none of his savvy,' Zococa complimented him drily.

Porter looked at the young bandit with disdain and hovered over Virgina Gunn as she pulled Polly even closer. 'I sure am gonna enjoy these females.'

'Release them, Tipah,' Zococa demanded as he held his snorting mount in check. 'Release them or I will kill you where you stand.'

'Mighty big talk for a man that's pumping blood all over his pretty horse,' Porter snarled like an enraged bear. His hands gripped the rifle. 'I reckon I'll take that stallion too. He sure don't need no dead master.'

Zococa stared at the last of the Comancheros. 'I will have to kill you, Tipah. You have brought it upon yourself.'

'You'll die trying, boy,' Porter threatened. He pushed the hand guard of his rifle up and down until the weapon was primed. 'I ain't no ordinary saddle tramp and you know that. I'll kill ya and that's a fact. Now git out of my way. I'm taking these yellow-haired females with me.'

Zococa could hear the sound of the two horses which were trailing him. His left hand moved above the grip of his holstered silver pistol. 'We have known each other for many years, *amigo*. I have to stop you, though. The Comancheros are finished. You are also finished.'

'But I got me ten men left.' Porter smiled as he took a step and glared up at the horseman.

'Zococa frowned. 'How? All your men are lying back there in pools of their own blood.'

Porter shook his head. 'Not all. I sent ten of my boys south with a herd of mavericks, Zococa. I'll just head on down to the border and rustle up a few more. The Comancheros ain't finished. Neither am I.'

Far behind him, Zococa could hear the hoofs of the two horses getting nearer as Tahoka and Gunn closed in on him. But they would not arrive in time, he silently told himself. The eyes of the handsome horseman darted to the tear-stained faces of the females before returning to Porter. It was as though a fuse had been ignited in his soul.

'Ya gonna draw that pretty little gun, Zococa?' Porter taunted. 'Ya got enough guts to find out which one of us is the fastest?'

'Your rifle is already cocked, Tipah,' Zococa remarked drily. 'I do not think our duel will be fair.'

'Not fair, huh?' Porter smiled. It was a humourless smile designed to destroy the other man's courage. 'Ain't that a crying shame?'

'So be it.' Zococa's fingers flexed. 'I await your pleasure, *amigo.*'

Then it happened. Faster than Zococa had imagined possible, Porter pivoted his entire body and squeezed the trigger of his Winchester. A blinding flash. A taste of gunsmoke.

Zococa's hand had only just pulled his pistol from its holster when he felt the impact as the rifle bullet hit him. He grunted in a cocktail of shock and pain. He felt himself roll back over his high cantle and fall. Before he crashed into the soil Zococa managed to cock and fire his pistol through the legs of his stallion.

A deafening sound of fury filled the air as Porter buckled and was knocked backwards. Porter steadied himself quickly though. He was not easily killed.

Both men had tasted each other's lead.

Zococa lay at the feet of the stallion. Tipah Porter staggered and cranked the mechanism of his rifle again. They both managed to fire once more.

Shafts of light and noise crossed paths.

Blood sprayed across the rockface as Porter felt his opponent's bullet rip a hole through him. Defiantly he pushed the guard of the carbine down and back up once more as he surveyed his target. The sunlight danced across the silver pistol as the wounded Zococa managed to get to his knees. His black jacket was now crimson. He blinked hard and saw his large sombrero on the ground beside him. He then looked up at the contemptuous Porter.

Both men fired again, sending rods of lethal lead across the distance which separated them. Both men's bullets found their mark. Zococa landed on his back. His pistol fell from his hand.

The Winchester dropped from Porter's grip. He turned and tried to step towards the saddled horses, but his legs failed him. He toppled face first into the dirt.

Tipah Porter was dead.

The two horses which had been following the tracks left by the stallion rode into the clearing. Both horsemen drew leather. Tahoka stared in horror at Zococa spread out on the ground beside his stallion. The Apache threw his leg over the neck of his gelding and rushed to his fallen friend.

Hal Gunn could not see anything but his wife and their daughter. He dismounted and ran to them.

FINALE

The acrid scent of gunsmoke drifted heavenwards as Hal Gunn led his wife and child away from the blood-stained scene. He had found them at last but he knew the cost of their salvation had been high. With her daughter clinging to her skirt Virgina Gunn held on to the bridle of the marshal's horse and watched her husband walk to where Zococa lay cradled in the arms of the mighty Tahoka, who was kneeling on the ground. Gunn had never before felt so emotional but for the first time in his life he was unashamed.

He knew the debt he owed the brutally wounded bandit. It was one he could never repay.

Gunn crouched down and looked into Zococa's wide-open eyes, then he cleared his throat.

'Thanks, Zococa,' the marshal whispered and shook his head sadly. 'Ya did it for me. Ya found and saved my wife and child and it's cost ya more than any man ought to have to pay, son.'

Zococa was badly hurt. His clothing was stained with the bloody evidence of the gruesome combat yet somehow he managed to force a smile as blood trickled from the corner of his mouth.

'It was an honour, *amigo*.' Zococa said.

'I was loco with grief but ya forced me to believe.' The star rider patted the bloodstained hand. 'Ya a damn fine man.'

'Bandit, *amigo*,' Zococa corrected.

Tahoka used his free hand to speak urgently to the bandit, but then felt his hand being stopped by the young bandit's own. 'Quiet, my little elephant. You chatter and worry too much. I know we have to go.'

The eyes of the Apache warrior looked straight into those of the marshal as Gunn raised himself back to his full height. Even without words the star rider knew what Tahoka was trying to convey. Gunn nodded to the huge man and then walked slowly back to his horse and his awaiting wife and daughter.

'Is he going to be OK, Daddy?' the small girl asked her father. 'I don't want him to die.'

Gunn's hand smoothed her golden hair but he was unable to answer.

Then unexpectedly little Polly broke away from her parents' sides and ran to where Zococa was being held in the kneeling Tahoka's muscular arms. She looked down at the handsome bandit with tear-filled eyes.

'I don't want ya to die, Zococa,' she sobbed. 'Please don't die.'

Somehow Zococa managed to reach his sombrero. He dragged it across the stained sand and covered his wounded body with its wide brim to shield his injuries from her.

He winked up at her.

'Do not shed tears for the great Zococa, my beautiful angel. I will be fine.'

'Ya promise?' Polly reached out and held his hand in her small fingers.

'*Sí*. I promise, my golden one.' Zococa smiled.

Polly blew a kiss to him and then turned and skipped back to where her proud parents waited.

Tahoka carefully lifted the limp Zococa off the ground and carried him to the pinto stallion. Like a mother with her newborn baby the huge Indian gently helped the bandit up on to his saddle, then climbed up behind him. Tahoka gathered up the reins with one hand as the other held Zococa firmly in place.

Hal Gunn walked to the stallion. His eyes looked at the blood which again was starting to flow from the bandit's hideous wounds. 'Ya hurt too bad to go riding, boy. Ya need a doctor. Hear me? Ya need a doctor.'

Zococa forced a frail smile. 'You forget that I am the great Zococa. I am a legend, *amigo*. My little rhinoceros will take me to one who can help mend my wounds. I will not die.'

'How can ya be so damn sure, Zococa?' Gunn felt his words choking him. 'How?'

Zococa looked at the small child and smiled at her as Tahoka tapped the sides of the tall pinto stallion and gently urged the horse to walk away. 'Because I promised the little golden angel, and Zococa never breaks a promise, *amigo*. Not to angels anyway.'

Gunn placed one arm around Virginia's shoulder and the other on the head of the waving Polly. They watched in awe as the Apache warrior guided the stallion back along the gulch, his black gelding trailing behind them.

'Who is he, Hal?' Virginia asked.

The star rider could see the bandit slump in Tahoka's arms as they rode between the trees. His heart began to sink.

'They call him Zococa,' Gunn managed to say.

'Do ya really think he'll be OK?' Virginia looked at her husband's face. 'I've never seen anyone survive when they've bin hurt that bad.'

The star rider squeezed her shoulder hard.

'Didn't ya hear him? He's a legend. Legends can't die.'